Emma's Engagement
Book 1 in Clover Creek Community
Kirsten Osbourne

Copyright © 2022 by Kirsten Osbourne

Unlimited Dreams Publishing

All rights reserved.

Cover design by Erin Dameron Hill/ EDH Graphics

No part of this book may be reproduced in any form or by any electronic or mechanical means including information storage and retrieval systems, without permission in writing from the author. The only exception is by a reviewer, who may quote short excerpts in a review.

This book is a work of fiction. Names, characters, places, and incidents either are products of the author's imagination or are used fictitiously. Any resemblance to actual persons, living or dead, events, or locales is entirely coincidental.

Kirsten Osbourne

Visit my website at www.kirstenandmorganna.com

Chapter One

Emma Williams wished her father could get the house he'd promised her mother built before winter, but there was just no time. Instead, they would winter in a log cabin. Thankfully, Pa had built a loft for her and her sisters. Only problem was it was for her and *her sisters*. She needed her own space sometimes. Especially now that she was being courted by the most handsome man in their entire community—Jared Appleby.

Emma had first developed a crush on Jared when they were still in Independence, Missouri, and she'd thought many times about approaching him to talk to him on their incredibly long journey, but Ma had told her over and over that ladies didn't pursue gentlemen. So, she'd waited for him to come to her, but it was a long wait.

But now, everything was wonderful between them. Tonight, she was cooking for him and his family for the first time ever, and she was a little nervous. She couldn't cook as well as her ma, but she'd been learning to cook since she was a young girl.

She was making a roast that her brother had brought her from one of the elk he had shot and butchered. She couldn't wait to see his face when he tasted it. Emma was the best cook out of the three girls in her family, and she couldn't wait for Jared to lavish her with praises about what a good cook she was.

She climbed down the stairs from the loft to see her mother stirring something over the fire. "I was going to start supper for the Applebys, Ma."

"You can build a firepit outside. It's chilly, but the fire will keep you warm, and I won't be looking over your shoulder telling you each step.

You must learn to cook on your own and not having me looking over your shoulder every time you make a meal."

Emma nodded. "Yes, Ma." She took the second large pot from its spot in one corner of the kitchen and put the roast into it. "I'll peel the potatoes and add them. I wish I knew how to bake bread."

"Your pa was never fond of my bread, so I quit making it years ago, when Roy was a small boy. I'm sure the Appleby family got used to not having bread on the trail." Ma looked up and smiled at her daughter. "You're every bit as good of a cook as I am. Stop being nervous about this."

"I just want Jared to be so pleased with my meal, he'll drop to one knee, and ask me to marry him right then!" Emma smiled dreamily as she thought about it. She would love to be married before winter and not have to keep sharing that silly loft. Besides, it would be fun for her and her brother to be married to siblings. Then their children would be cousins on both sides.

While she cooked, she fantasized about what a perfect life she'd have with Jared. He was such a sweet man, and he'd lost his mother shortly before they arrived in Clover Creek. She felt terrible for him, but at least he had a sister to cook for them. Now that his sister, Henrietta, was married to her brother, Roy, he and his father and brothers had no one to cook for them. So, she was going to cook for them that evening. Hopefully, he would think even more of her skills as a wife after she'd done so.

As she was cooking, Jared walked down the hill. "Hello," she said, looking down and blushing. He'd asked to court her, but they hadn't kissed yet. She hoped she could quit pretending to be shy around him after they kissed. Her ma said it was necessary at least until there had been some physical display of affection, but she also said never to tell her pa if there was a physical display of affection. Her ma confused her at times.

She had the meat in the pot, as well as the carrots, and she wanted him to be surprised at the meal she was making, so she hurried to him, away from the fire.

He smiled at her, his eyes roaming over her face. "You look beautiful this afternoon," he said.

She smiled and remembered to look down in embarrassment. "Thank you."

"I just wanted to make sure you are still making supper for us tonight. I cannot wait to taste your cooking. Roy told me you were the best cook of all his sisters. My expectations are high." He smiled at her, wishing he could reach out and touch her, but he knew better. Her ma was probably watching them. He would be if she was his daughter.

Then his mind wandered to making daughters with her. Or sons. It didn't really matter as long as they were making babies. He wasn't fussy.

She smiled demurely—at least she hoped her smile was demure. "I hope I can live up to your expectations."

"Me too! I can come down and help you carry supper up to us if you'd like."

She nodded. "That would be wonderful. The pot is heavy to carry that far uphill."

"Then I will be here to escort you." He took her hand and bowed over it, brushing his lips across the back of her hand. "You shall be my damsel in distress for the evening."

She nodded. "I can't wait. I don't think I've ever talked to your brothers or your pa. I adore Henri though."

"Henri is pretty great for a kid sister," he said, grinning. "I'll be down around six."

"I'll be here." Emma watched Jared as he walked away. She knew she wasn't supposed to be curious about a man's body, but Jared had such broad shoulders, and his bottom looked nice in his work pants.

She had to force herself to stop looking and turn around and get back to cooking. She hoped her roast turned out just as well as her ma's always did.

On his way up the hill, Jared ran into Henri who was kindly taking them supper. When he explained that Emma was cooking for them, the look on her face made him nervous. But if she was the best cook of her family, how bad could she really be?

He took the food she'd made for their supper, carrying it to his pa's cabin. They'd all agreed to eat together, and Henri made fresh bread daily, which was nice. He knew a lot of women had a hard time making bread over the open fire. Henri followed him into the cabin with a full ten loaves of bread. "That might be enough to hold you until I make more bread," Henri said, smiling sweetly at him.

He chuckled. "Not if Bastian sees it before Pa does. Pa always hides some of it, so Bastian won't eat it all at once."

Henri laughed, shaking her head. "I'm going to make our supper now. I hope you have a good evening."

"I'm sure we will. She was already cooking when I went over there a few minutes ago."

"I'm sure it will be wonderful." Henri left and headed back down the hill to where she shared a cabin with Roy, her new husband, and Emma's brother. Roy had chosen to build a house that was only a two-minute walk from his pa, as had he and his brothers. It would be nice to be able to plan out their work schedules more easily.

Jared was the oldest brother in the Appleby family. He and his brothers had agreed to start a ranch with their pa. So, while they'd all filed a claim for their own property, they planned to start one huge ranch across all the land together.

Unfortunately, Jared's was the last of the three cabins he, his father, and his brothers would build before winter. He was getting his own, because he was already very certain that Emma would be his bride, and he wanted to marry before winter set in. He liked the idea of staying in the house during a blizzard with his new bride. Hopefully he could even convince her that clothing was optional, but she seemed much too shy for that.

He was sleeping on the floor of Pa's cabin yet. He could probably sleep up in the loft, where a cozy space had been made for Henri, but it just didn't appeal. They'd built it for Henri's height, and the bed had been just the right size for a small woman, not a large man.

Jared headed back toward the cabin they were building for him and Emma. He would try to build her a house next summer, but a small cabin would have to do for the winter. But a house would need to be built before the babies started coming.

WHEN JARED SHOWED UP to help her carry the food up the hill, she put the lid on the pot with the roast and potatoes. She hoped he liked the food as much as her family did.

"I didn't have time to make a dessert," she said. Honestly, though, her ma had never really taught her to do any baking. Ma had always said it was much too complicated.

He took the pot from her and offered her his free arm, which she readily took. She could feel the muscles of his arm through his sleeve, and it made her tingle a little. Wearing her thickest sweater, she shivered a little. While it had been warm during the day, it was so cold at night there. Pa said it was from the high elevation, but she didn't know much about it.

"How is your cabin coming?" she asked. He'd told her that he was building a cabin and hoped she'd be all right with wintering in it until he could build a real house next summer.

He sighed. "Much slower than I would like. It feels like it's taking three times as long as Pa's did."

"But yours is smaller," she said with a frown. That made no sense to her.

"Yeah, but we had four of us building Pa's. Two of us keep having to work on building a shelter for the cattle. They need to be warm this winter as well."

She nodded. "As soon as Roy gets enough food in for us for the winter, he's going to help Pa build a barn as well. It's just hard to choose what the most important thing is."

"It is. We'll all be hunting as soon as my cabin is built." Jared gave her a look that made her tummy quiver. "Our cabin."

Emma smiled happily, forgetting for a moment to be shy. "I'm excited to be able to share it with you. Even if it must be for two years, I don't care. We'll be close together in it, which will be nice."

Jared grinned. "I like the idea of that."

He opened the cabin door to his pa's house for her. He wished for a moment that they had the same house they'd had in Indiana, but he knew no one in the community had anything that seemed even a bit like wealth. Perhaps some were richer than others, but you could never tell by looking around at the log cabins that were being erected all over the place.

Emma preceded him into the house and looked around, smiling. "What's that?" she asked, looking at the pot of food he'd brought up the hill earlier, and the huge pile of bread loaves.

"Henri didn't know you were cooking for us tonight, so she brought supper up for us. We'll have it for lunch tomorrow or supper tomorrow night. But we can have bread with what you made tonight. And butter. We don't have much butter left, but Henri said Roy is building her a butter churn. She'll be making butter for us then, so we can eat some now, knowing it will be replaced soon."

"Henri seems like she knows so much about cooking."

Jared nodded. "Oh, she does. Ma was a wonderful cook, but Henri is even better."

"She is?" Emma felt a bit intimidated by how everyone bragged about Henri so much.

Jared's father and brothers came in then, stomping their feet. Without Henri there to clean for them, they were being a great deal more careful about the messes they made.

Bastian sniffed the air. "Something smells good!"

Sam nodded. "Oh, yeah. It will be great to have another good cook in the family. Maybe you and Henri can trade off feeding us."

Deep in the pit of her stomach, Emma worried that the good smell was coming from the food Henri had brought and had nothing to do with her cooking. "I hope it tastes as good as it smells," she said, her voice small. All these men were used to excellent cooking, and she knew she wasn't as knowledgeable as Henri was.

Jared set the pot on the edge of the fireplace, and sat down at the table, waiting for his future bride to show off her cooking prowess. His father and brothers joined him. "Henri keeps the plates on that shelf there," Jared said, pointing helpfully to the corner of the room. He was hungry and ready for the food to be served.

Emma smiled, walked to the corner, and quickly put the cutlery on the table. At least she knew she was doing that correctly. Then she took five plates, and filled each with her roast, potatoes, and carrots. "Oh, and Henri brought bread." She hurried to the bread and brought back two loaves along with the butter and a knife to cut the bread.

Taking her seat to Jared's right, she looked at the men. She didn't know if they prayed before every meal or not, but her family did. No one was eating, so she bowed her head, waiting for someone to pray.

Jared exchanged looks with his father and brothers. They were all looking at the dried-out meat and burnt potatoes and carrots, just as he was. Finally, he bowed his head, saying a prayer for the meal provided.

While his father and brothers waited, Jared bravely cut off a bite of the meat, sticking it in his mouth and saying a silent prayer it wasn't as bad as it looked. It was worse. So much worse.

Beside him, Emma was happily eating her meal. "Oh, this turned out better than ever!" she said.

"Did you forget to put water in it?" Jared asked softly.

"Oh, I never put water in it. It would make the meat less flavorful."

"But it would be moist and juicy," Bastian said, keeping his voice soft as well. He knew little about cooking, but even he knew you needed to put water on roast.

Emma frowned. "It tastes like it's supposed to taste."

The other men each ate a bite of the roast, and then tried the carrots and potatoes. Each one chewed the bite and swallowed it.

Finally, Bastian said, "This isn't what smelled so good. Is this a joke? Do you have our real meal somewhere else?" He got up and started looking. "Oh, you're a real tease. I found our real meal." He laughed softly. "You shouldn't play tricks on us like that."

Bastian put the food Henri had provided on one end of the table, and Mr. Appleby served everyone more food on top of what they had. Emma was mortified, but she didn't correct Bastian's assumption that she'd been playing a trick on them. The worst part of it all was that Jared didn't correct them either, but he did pass his and her plates down to his father to fill.

Emma looked at the meal, realizing it was the exact same thing she'd made, but it looked so different. This roast looked moist and smelled so much better than anything she'd ever cooked. When she took her first bite, she almost moaned in pleasure. No wonder they bragged about Henri's cooking. She was a marvel!

They all cut up the bread and spread butter, each of them enjoying the meal now that they weren't eating hers.

After they'd finished eating, Jared stood. "I'll walk you home. Would you mind leaving the pot with the second roast here, so we can have what's left for lunch tomorrow?"

Emma shook her head, absolutely mortified. "Of course not."

Jared took the pot with the roast she had made and set the lid back on it. "I'll be back to sleep on your floor in a bit, Pa."

Pa nodded. "I'm going to eat a little more. Your sweet girl is as good of a cook as our Henri. I think we're all going to be happy to have two good cooks in the family."

Jared waited until they were beyond hearing distance of the house. "Has no one taught you to cook properly?" he asked softly.

Emma shook her head, bursting into tears. "I thought I *was* cooking properly. This is how my ma does it!"

Jared felt terrible that he'd made her cry. "It doesn't change how I feel about you, but I need to ask you a favor before we can marry."

"What's that?" she asked, surprised he still wanted to court her.

"Will you go to my sister for cooking lessons? I know it's a lot to ask, but she can show you a few tricks that will make your meals as good as hers in no time."

Emma cried harder, but she nodded. "I'll learn anything she's willing to teach me."

Jared smiled, stopping, and setting the pot on the ground. He pulled Emma into his arms, and held her, stroking her hair. "I'm sorry you were embarrassed tonight. My family will never know, but I'll need you to improve. Your mother and sisters should probably go with you."

Emma nodded, burying her face in his shoulder. "I'm sorry."

"Hey, you did nothing wrong. Your mother should be flogged for not teaching you any better, but you cooked the way you were taught." He cupped her cheeks in his hands, and leaned down, brushing a kiss across her lips for the first time. "You're still the girl I want to marry."

She pulled a little back, smiling through her tears. "You've never kissed me before."

"Well, I hope you like my kisses, because they're going to be coming pretty often!"

When he left her at the front door, she dumped the food out onto the ground. Now that she knew it wasn't good enough to really eat, and having tasted the difference, she saw no reason to save it.

Chapter Two

All the following day, Emma wallowed. She didn't want to help with chores, but she did, doing it silently. She knew she was being mopey, and it wasn't an attractive quality in a young lady, but at that moment, she didn't care. Her whole world had just turned upside down. What she'd believed her entire life had been very wrong.

She wiped off the table after the noon meal, which tasted much like the one she'd made for the Applebys the previous evening. When she walked outside to help with hanging the laundry, she spotted the food she'd dumped out. With all the wildlife around, the food should have been gone. It was telling that it wasn't.

No one asked her about the food on the ground, and she said nothing. Emma wanted to run to her brother's cabin to talk to Henri, but she'd wait until they came over for supper that night. No point in doing otherwise. By the time Henri had eaten her mother's cooking, she knew the other girl would be looking down on her anyway.

How humiliating! She'd believed she was great at keeping house, and here she was, incapable of cooking a decent meal. She hoped she could learn as quickly as Jared seemed to think she should.

Thinking of him made her smile, but just a smidge. His kiss the night before had left her wanting so much more from him. She looked forward to the day when they could share a marriage bed.

When her mother started a roast for supper, Emma talked to her softly, so her sisters wouldn't hear. "Ma, you're supposed to put water in with a roast, so it doesn't come out dry. And it makes the potatoes and carrots cook better as well."

Ma straightened her back up. "Do you realize your pa said the same thing to me this morning, and he told me I had to do it that way from now on? Did you have something to do with that?"

Emma's eyes widened. She shook her head. "I didn't, Ma. I swear." She quickly explained what had happened at the Appleby house the night before. "I've never been so embarrassed in my life."

Ma shook her head. "There are dozens of ways to cook things. There is no right way. I'm not pleased that family is putting ideas like that in your head."

"Sorry, Ma." Emma decided she wouldn't speak until spoken to for the rest of the day. It would give her a little more time to stew in her embarrassment.

When Roy and Henri arrived for supper that evening, Henri brought some of the fresh bread she made daily. Emma asked at one point if Henri would teach her to cook, and then she returned to her silence. Emma just hoped she hadn't learned so many bad habits she'd never be able to cook a decent meal.

Henri worked with Emma on cooking all day Saturday before her family arrived to have supper. Henri bragged about how well she'd done to her family, and Henri felt as if she'd done something truly remarkable.

Emma, Ma, and Emma's sisters Abigail and Barbara spent all day Monday learning to make a turkey feast, and the surprise part for Emma at the end of the day was that everyone enjoyed it. They'd had turkey, stuffing, mashed potatoes, pies and everything else they could find that went with turkey. It was a fun day with all of them working together.

On Tuesday, Ma, Emma, Abigail, and Barbara were all taking cooking lessons from Henri again. Emma wished she didn't have to share her lessons with her sisters, but it made sense. They'd been taught to cook the same way she had.

Emma had never realized how young Ma had been when her own mother died. There'd been no time for Ma to learn to cook properly, which explained why she'd never taught Emma to do better than she had.

Emma was truly excited to learn to cook from someone who was as good a cook as Henri was.

As Henri taught them, Ma would watch, and then run outside to a fire she'd started and do the same thing with the meal she was cooking. Emma helped as much as she could, but it seemed everyone thought Ma learning to cook was a higher priority than Emma learning.

Halfway through the day, Emma found her answer. "Henri, would it be all right if I cooked for your family? Then I could follow what you do as well."

Henri looked at Emma with a huge grin on her face. "I think that's a brilliant idea. It's better if everyone can be hands on as they learn."

Emma grinned. "Thanks. I'm going to go build another fire."

Barbara sighed. "What can I do?"

"You can help your sister gather some wood for kindling, and then you can help her carry what she needs for supper outside," Henri said to the youngest of the Williams sisters.

Abigail had helped whenever she could. She'd even kneaded bread, while Barbara had looked confused as to what she should be doing. "Can I just keep helping where I see I can?" Abigail asked softly. She was the middle sister and was much shyer than the other two.

Henri nodded. "You're doing great. After Emma marries Jared, you'll have plenty of time to learn to cook yourself."

Abigail nodded. "Emma needs to learn first so she can get married."

"I agree."

The ladies had a fun day, learning and working together. At the end of the day, they all tried a small bit of all three meals. Emma was surprised that hers tasted almost as good as Henri's, though Ma's wasn't quite as good as either of the others. Emma knew her ma hated to cook with everything inside her, but she'd taught them to clean and sew beautifully.

And Emma knew how to take care of a baby with two younger sisters, and she had helped with some of the babies along the trail. It had been fun for her to visualize the babies and imagine they were hers and Jared's.

"I'm going to carry this up the hill to your family," Emma said, pleased with her own cooking, and finally being certain her family would be pleased as well.

Henri smiled. "They're going to love it." She looked for the bread she'd baked and wrapped four loaves in a large cloth. "I'll walk with you."

"Thank you!" Emma said.

"We'll switch the pot back and forth. It's heavy for one person."

"Your help will be most welcome."

"Do you think they'll like the rice and stew we made?" Emma asked.

"They have always liked it when I made it, and yours was just as good as mine."

Emma knew it wasn't true, but she took the compliment. "Learning to season things seems to be the hardest," she said. "I couldn't quite get the exact taste of yours."

Henri chuckled. "I never have the exact same taste twice. I measure when I bake, but not so much when I cook. You'll see what I mean as you get more confident with yourself."

"Please don't tell anyone the supper we all ate on Thursday night was cooked by you," Emma said softly. "Bastian looked at my meal and decided it must have been a trick I was playing on them. Jared knew better, but he didn't say anything."

"Don't worry. I know better than telling the family my sister couldn't cook until this weekend."

Emma felt proud to be called Henri's sister. "Thank you. I'm glad you're here and willing to help so much."

"This year has been so difficult for all of us. We women will have much more difficult jobs out west than we ever did in the east. We all need to learn together and work together to get things done. For instance, I see the little butterfly on the collar of your dress. Did you make that?" Henri asked.

Emma nodded. "Ma sews really well, and she's taught me."

"I would love to learn to do something like that. Perhaps you could teach me after I teach you to cook."

Emma was thrilled to have something to offer. "Did you make the dress you're wearing?" she asked.

"I did," Henri replied. "But sewing is difficult, tedious work for me. I prefer to cook."

"Your new curtains look beautiful!" Emma said.

"I can sew a straight line really well..."

Emma laughed. "I'll teach you everything I know. I'm excited that we can learn together."

"So am I!" Henri said. "Let me take the pot. We're about halfway. You take the bread."

As they exchanged, Emma shook her arm a little. "I don't know how you carry so many meals up here to your family. That's hard work!"

"Usually, one of my brothers will meet me coming up the hill or they'll just come by at the end of their workday and take it up. They could eat with us, but they seem to want us to have more privacy as newlyweds."

Emma bit her lip, wondering how indelicate it would be for her to ask the question on her mind. "Do you like...sharing a bed with my brother?"

Henri blushed. "I do."

When it was obvious to Emma the subject bothered Henri, she decided not to ask anything more on the topic, so she quickly changed the subject. "How many meals should I go into a marriage being able to make?"

Henri thought for a moment before answering. "You can make two breakfasts now. You'll want to learn more, but if you just alternate the two, Jared will be happy. He can make scrambled eggs and bacon as well, so he can show you those things if you want. You don't only have a couple of things you can make now, though. You can make gravy from jerky and put it over rice. Or mashed potatoes. So that's two meals. You can make a beautiful roast. You can make stew. Tomorrow, I'll teach you to make a filling soup. I think you could marry Jared this week and be just fine. We'll keep working on things until you know just what you're doing."

"Jared told me I should have you teach me to cook," Emma said. "I was so embarrassed I couldn't quit crying, and he didn't get angry. He just told me what I should do to get better. He was very kind."

Henri smiled. "I'm glad. I'd have to say something otherwise. Do you think the two of you will marry soon?"

"Maybe after he eats my stew tonight."

Henri giggled. "I don't always make rice with my stew, but rice keeps for a long time. By serving the stew with rice and bread, it makes the meal stretch much further. I have little things like that I'll teach you as we go along. You need to be able to make food stretch as far as it possibly can."

"Will you teach me how to salt meat?" Emma asked. "Ma only knows how to dry it, and I would like a variety."

"I've made a deal with your ma that she will make my jerky, and I'll salt meat for her. Then we'll all have a variety through the winter. But yes, I'd be thrilled to teach you to salt meat. We do need more jars, though."

"Where will we get some?" Emma asked. Now that they were in Oregon Territory, there was no real place for them to shop. She didn't know what she would be able to do about jars.

"I'm not sure. I know Ma told the boys to each bring a couple of dozen because their wagons weren't quite as full as ours, but I'm not sure they listened." Henri shook her head. "Men rarely listen!"

Emma laughed. "If they did bring them, will they let us use them?"

Henri nodded. "I shouldn't have borrowed from your ma before asking them anyway. But they would have brought them expecting someone else to use them."

Henri pushed the door open and stepped into the house, putting the huge pot they'd carried next to the fireplace so it could be heated up. "I wish someone was here!"

"Someone like me?" Jared asked, his voice even deeper than Emma remembered. His voice made her tingle all over.

Before Emma could respond, Henri said, "You'll do."

Jared ignored his sister. "What are you doing here?" he asked Emma.

"Henri has spent the whole weekend teaching me to cook. I made your supper tonight, and though it's not as good as Henri's, I think everyone will like it."

Jared raised an eyebrow. "It sure smells good. You made it?" He had to be certain because her last meal had been such a fiasco.

Emma nodded. "I did. And I helped make the bread today as well."

He smiled happily. "My cabin was finished today. Do you think you need another week or two to learn to cook? Or could we get married tomorrow?"

She bit her lip. "I think we could get married tomorrow. I'll keep learning from Henri as we go. Her house isn't far."

"It's about a ten-minute walk. I think that will usually be okay." He thought for a moment. "I'm going to make you a sled. Sled down the hill on it every day, and I'll bring it back up at the end of my day. I don't want you slipping on the ice."

She laughed, thinking for a moment he was joking. "Sure, I'll sled down to her."

"I'm serious. It'll be easier than slipping and falling. Or would you rather I made you snowshoes?"

Henri responded for Emma. "She needs both. I love that we live so close, but that hill is awfully steep."

"Both it is!" Jared said. "I'm trying to plan my wedding here, dear sister."

"What do you want me to do? I can go outside and wait while you two make your plans. Or I can just go home."

"Wait outside. We'll talk fast."

Henri hmphed under her breath, but she went out the door.

Jared took both of Emma's hands in his. "I asked your pa at church on Sunday. He's agreed if you would like to be my wife."

Emma's heart skipped a beat. She'd known it was coming, but it was so special. "I'd love to be your wife." She'd remember this moment for the rest of her life and tell her daughters all about how their pa had asked her to marry him.

Jared gathered her close and kissed her in a much more passionate way than he had the first time. Her stomach was on fire before he ended the kiss. "I'll come get you tomorrow morning. We're taking my horse because it will be better than hitching up a wagon. I'm worried we'll get snow any day."

"My pa's been saying the same thing. I'll be ready."

"I don't think we should have anyone go along with us," he said. "We can't ask people to slow down their work. Winter is too close."

"I thought I smelled snow this morning."

"My ma could always tell when snow was about to fall by the smell." She grinned. "My ma says it's nonsense."

"Be ready for me at eight. I'll talk to Pastor Jed tonight." Never in his life had he referred to a pastor by his first name, but it just seemed right with Jed. They were around the same age, and Jed was a man who was easy to approach.

"I'll be waiting for you. I can't wait to see my new home!"

He laughed. "It looks like all the other homes around here. You'll have to use my pa's cellar."

"Henri was going to teach me to salt meat tomorrow..."

"You can still go. I even brought two dozen jars at my mother's insistence. I think my brothers did too."

"We were going to ask you that..."

"Now you don't have to." Jared sighed. Just one more night of sleeping alone, and he would have his sweet Emma in his arms. With one last kiss, he went outside. "You two walk home together. I want to put a couple of last-minute touches on the cabin so it will be ready for my beautiful bride."

Henri grinned at Emma. "I'm so excited we're going to be double sisters."

Emma laughed. "And our children will be double cousins. Life sure does take some strange twists and turns, doesn't it?"

"It does!" As they walked down the hill, Emma felt like she was floating on air.

"Jared won't change his mind if he hates the meal I cooked this evening, will he?" she asked.

Henri shook her head. "No, he won't. He's not that kind of man."

"I sure hope you're right. I still worry about my cooking and what he expects in the way of food. I need to learn fast and get your receipts written down. We didn't write anything Monday or today!"

"You only need exact receipts for baking. The kind of cooking we did yesterday and today, other than the pie crusts, was just throwing things into the pot as we went along. You'll see how easy it is."

Emma nodded. "I sure hope you're right."

Chapter Three

Emma was up earlier than usual the next morning. She had so much nervous energy. She wanted to be Jared's wife more than anything, but she worried she wouldn't be a good enough wife to him.

She only ate a few bites at breakfast and drank a couple of cups of coffee, which was unusual for her. She wasn't a fan of coffee, but her father was insisting they still drink either coffee or tea. He didn't trust the water they were drinking. He claimed that everyone who had gotten sick along the trail hadn't drunk coffee or tea, and he wasn't going to see his family take as ill as the others.

She had no idea if he was right or wrong about drinking coffee or tea, but she knew she had to obey her father. It was as simple as that. And in a few hours, she would promise to obey Jared for the rest of her life. Emma had to wonder if it was really necessary for women to obey men, or if it was something some man had come up with and all others had agreed with. She felt as if she had a mind that could think as well as any man's.

Not that she would ever think of disobeying either her father or her husband. She just wondered why men thought women had to be obedient.

She helped her mother with the morning dishes and put all the things she brought west in a hope chest back into the chest. Her brother had made room in his wagon for her valuable things, and she was pleased she would have them.

She had collected dishes, pots and pans, linens, and she'd even made a special dress to be married in before leaving Iowa. The dress had been taken in the previous evening. She hadn't realized just how much leaner she was after her two thousand mile walk across the west.

Pa and Roy were outside when Jared arrived, and they hoisted the chest into the back of Jared's wagon. "Why did you bring a wagon?" she called. "I thought we were going to ride a horse." She'd been looking forward to clinging to him as they drove down the hill and to the church.

"My pa told me that was the most ridiculous thing he'd ever heard, and a lady should be driven to her wedding, not ride a horse. I wasn't going to argue with him, so I'm here in a wagon."

Jared was at her side when he finished speaking. "You look beautiful today. I can't wait to begin our life together."

Emma smiled. "I guess supper was to your satisfaction last night then?"

He laughed. "My whole family thought Henri had made it, and when I told them it was you, they weren't even surprised."

"Well, then I'm happy. I'm supposed to go to Henri's house as soon as I settle in. Apparently, my brother got another elk yesterday, and I'm going to learn how to salt meat. We'll have it for our winter."

He handed her up into the wagon. "That's wonderful. But for just the next hour, let's not even think about our winter preparations. Let's just be happy and celebrate the fact we're getting married."

She turned and waved to her brother and father, feeling as if she'd never see them again, which was ridiculous. They lived just a few-minute walk down the hill, and apparently, she was going to have snowshoes and a sled before winter to get down and up the hill with.

As they drove, she said, "I can't believe how nervous I am. I want nothing more than to be your wife, but my stomach is all aflutter. I'm about to promise to love you and obey you for the rest of our lives. Make sure you don't tell me to do anything stupid, all right?"

He laughed. "I wouldn't. If you're worried, though, we can postpone this for a few more days." Jared truly wasn't sure if he could wait that long before marrying her, but if it would calm her nerves, her feelings must come first. It was something he'd been taught since he was a child.

"No, I don't want to wait, but that doesn't make me any less nervous." When he stopped the wagon in front of the church the entire community had erected just weeks before, she moved toward the edge to jump down as she had so often, but he was there with his hands raised to help her down. It was like he believed she really was a lady, when she felt like a little girl inside. With his hands at her waist, he lifted her down from the wagon, and she couldn't help but smile.

Inside the church, Pastor Jed and his wife Hannah were there, as was Fiona Jefferson, a girl Emma knew from the trail. She smiled at the other ladies as she approached the front of the church. She remembered Fiona was the daughter of Mr. and Mrs. Jefferson who planned to farm there. They had a plot of land just south of the church, whereas Emma and Jared's families had chosen land just north of the church. The church itself they'd built right there on the trail. Then the next wagon trains who came through could worship with them if they had a desire to.

Jared and Emma took their places in front of Pastor Jed, and Emma took a deep breath. She couldn't believe how very nervous she was to marry the man she'd been dreaming of marrying for well over two thousand miles.

The pastor's kind eyes looked at them both. "Are you ready?" he asked softly.

Emma nodded.

And so, the wedding began.

When it was time for Jared to kiss his new bride, he pulled her to him, and his kiss was much more passionate and more exciting than she thought was proper for a church. He didn't break off until the pastor cleared his throat.

Emma was dazed as he broke the kiss, and she swayed a little on her feet. Being married to her Jared would never be boring. She looked up into his eyes and thought for a moment about pulling his head down for one more kiss, but she could feel people's eyes on her.

Instead, she walked over to Mrs. Scott and Fiona. "Thanks for being the witnesses for our wedding."

Hannah laughed, slowly getting to her feet. "I will always be happy to do what I can for you. It looks like you've found true happiness with Jared. Isn't he the eldest of the Appleby boys?"

"Yes, he is," Emma agreed. "You look like that babe's going to be born any day!"

"Oh, don't say that! The doc and Mrs. Mitchell agree that it'll be at least another month. I've been sewing up a storm since we finally arrived here. I love that our home is right here in the church for now, but I hope one day, I'll be raising children in a real house."

"How many children do you want?" Emma asked.

"As many as the Lord gives me."

"Perfect answer for a pastor's wife," Fiona said. "I want an even dozen, but we're running out of eligible men around here. I don't want to have to start looking to the Indians to find a husband."

The three women laughed at that. "I hope it doesn't come to that," Emma said. "Remember Jared's got two younger brothers."

Fiona shook her head. "That Bastian looks like he'd be big trouble. Samuel, though...he's quieter, which might be scarier even. You don't know what to expect from him. No, I think I'll keep my eyes off those Appleby boys."

Emma laughed. "Well, if you change your mind, I'm happy to provide an introduction."

"I don't think you're supposed to be trying to be a matchmaker on your wedding day. Go on and be happy!" Fiona said, waving Emma away.

Hannah hugged Emma. "Be happy, my friend."

Emma had tears in her eyes as she turned away. She wasn't so certain about Fiona, but Hannah had been very sincere in her instructions to be happy. Emma would do all she could to follow those instructions.

Out in the wagon, they headed up to where the hill leveled off, where her parents and brother had settled, and then up to the next part of the hill where her in-laws had settled. It would be good to be as close to family as she was, but also enough apart that they would have the privacy a newlywed couple required.

He drove her in front of a small log cabin, much like her brother's, and he walked around, caught her by the waist, and kissed her while she dangled there in mid-air before setting her on the ground.

"I have to get to your sister's to help her with the salting of the meat," she said, wishing she could beg him to go inside so they could consummate the marriage. But she was an adult now, and it was important that she learned to work before she played.

He nodded. "I need to get the horses in the barn. It was finished a couple of days ago. It's big enough for our herd for this winter, though it's a little lopsided. Next year we'll have to build a real one. Maybe someone will start a sawmill. We can use one."

"Wouldn't it be nice if we could have real houses and not just log cabins?" she asked, thinking far into the future.

He frowned a bit. "I hope you'll be happy here in the meantime."

She smiled. "If I'm with you, I can't imagine being anything but happy."

He leaned down and kissed her one more time. "I'll see you at suppertime. I'll be eating the rest of that stew with my father and brothers while you learn with Henri."

"All right. I'm sure Henri and I will come up with something delicious." As Emma walked down the hill toward Henri and Roy's cabin, she realized she didn't feel any different. She was a married woman now, and she'd expected to suddenly feel all grown up and ready to conquer the world when she was married, but she still felt like plain old Emma Williams.

When she got to Henri's, she was surprised that her mother and sisters were there and there was lunch on the table for all five of them. "What's this?" she asked.

Henri smiled. "We thought a wedding lunch with just us ladies would be nice. And we all forgot about learning to churn butter yesterday, so your sisters will stay, and the four of us will take turns at the butter churn, and I'll teach you about salting meat. Your mother has taken a share, and she's going to spend the afternoon in a quiet house, making her jerky. But first, lunch."

It was the same meal Henri had taught Emma to make for lunch just Saturday. It was a jerky based gravy and served over rice. But Emma saw it had been made over mashed potatoes. She was certain Henri was trying to show her how to serve variations of each meal.

"Well, this is lovely. Thank you all."

Instead of letting Emma help serve, her sisters and Henri served her mother and herself. The meal was wonderful, and full of laughter. "Why do we never just take time to enjoy each other?" Emma asked.

"There's never any time," Ma told her. "But there will be here in the west. There will be lots of hard work, of course, but we'll also have time to visit with one another and share our days."

Henri nodded. "It seems so strange to settle into a new town, where we already know everyone, doesn't it?"

Emma nodded. "Fiona Jefferson was at the church this morning, and I thought the same thing. We just started a settlement with people that already feel like friends and family. I know I would have written to so many people if we'd settled apart, but now we can all just live in the same area happily."

Her mother nodded and smiled, waiting until everyone was seated. "I'll pray."

Every head bowed, and her mother thanked God for the meal and for sending a wonderful family into their lives, thanking God for her two new children, Henri and Jared.

When they raised their heads, Henri had a couple of tears on her cheeks. "I feel honored to be part of your family," she said softly.

They ate their meal slowly and when they were finished, Barbara and Abigail got up and brought something they'd hidden out of sight before Emma arrived. "A cake?" she asked, excited. "We never have cake!"

Ma laughed. "I know how to make one now, so you won't be able to say that any longer."

Emma was thrilled that her mother was taking to the new cooking lessons so well, even though she knew her mother hated to cook more than anything. After the cake, her mother pulled something out from under one of Henri's pillows. "I started this when I realized you and Jared would be courting."

It was a beautiful nightgown with lace all over the bodice, and it was sleeveless. It looked positively indecent to Emma, who stared at it in shock. "Wear this tonight," her mother said, saying nothing more.

"Yes, Ma," Emma said softly. How strange it was to have her mother make something that looked like a loose woman should wear it. It was beautiful, and she knew Jared would love it, but it still surprised her. Had Ma once worn something like that for Pa?

Henri eyed the nightgown. "Oh, that's so beautiful, Mrs. Williams. I wish I had the talent to sew as well as you do."

Ma Williams smiled. "I was hoping you'd say something like that." She walked to the bed and pulled out a nightgown that was very similar to Emma's. "I made this for you for your wedding night, but I didn't know if you would feel comfortable wearing it. I brought it today, hoping you would like Emma's."

Henri's eyes filled with tears again. "It's beautiful. Thank you so much!"

"When you finish the cooking lessons and we can all feed our menfolk, would you allow me to teach you some of my sewing tricks?" Ma asked.

Henri nodded emphatically. "I can't think of anything I'd like more. Maybe we could do a cooking lesson Mondays, a sewing lesson Tuesdays, and a baking lesson on Thursdays. I heard a rumor that the church is going to start a regular quilting circle every Thursday, and I think we should all be part of that. I hadn't realized just how many people on the trail with us that I only knew by sight. I don't know anything about them, and we're spending our lives together in this little community. I think it will be a great way for us all to get to know one another."

"I think so too!" Ma said. "Are children welcome, or only married ladies?"

Henri laughed. "If the married ladies are going, who will watch the children if they can't come?"

"That's a very good point," Emma said. "Do you know Fiona Jefferson very well?"

Everyone looked at one another and shook their heads. "No, not at all. We stayed to ourselves too much on that trail," Ma said.

Abigail nodded at that. "We really did."

"Well, she was one of the witnesses to my marriage today, and she said something that surprised me. She wants an even dozen children, and she talked like she planned to have exactly that many, no more, no less."

Henri nodded. "I talked to her a few times. She seems to know exactly what she wants out of life in a way that is odd for a woman. I must wonder how her future husband will feel about her."

"I hope he'll love her, despite how odd she seems to me," Emma said. She couldn't imagine being in a marriage with a man who didn't love her. Though, she was sitting at the table on her wedding day, realizing she and Jared had never said they loved one another. How odd.

Ma stood up. "I'm going to go home and make this exact thing for supper because I know how to make it now. And I'll do it over rice.

Thanks for giving me instructions on the correct way to make rice. I don't know why I thought I was supposed to fry it up."

"Always happy to help when I can, Mrs. Williams," Henri said, getting to her feet to embrace her mother-in-law. "Thank you for the beautiful gown."

"You're very welcome," Ma said. "You girls finish the butter and then come home."

Abigail nodded. "Yes, Ma."

Barbara didn't respond, but that was typical for Barbara. She was thinking about other things.

"All right," Henri said, getting to her feet. "Let's get this butter churned, and then we'll do a bit of the meat. We spent longer on lunch than planned, but we couldn't not have a wedding celebration."

Henri showed the girls how to skim the cream off the top of the milk, and then she poured the cream into her new butter churn. "Then all we do is take turns stirring it with this huge paddle," she explained. "The longer you stir, the harder it gets, not only because your arms get tired, but also because the cream is getting thicker and turning into butter. Back home, Ma and I had started buying it at the store in town. I'm not looking forward to having to make my own again."

Barbara took the first turn. "I think I'm going to like churning butter."

Henri nodded, but she looked skeptical.

"Now we need to salt the meat," Henri said. "We're going to go out and cut off roast size pieces of the meat. Your family will need a larger size, as will my family. You and I will need smaller roasts."

Emma nodded. "All right." She took a long piece of wood out to the elk carcass hanging upside down from a tree, and she cut off a roast sized portion. "Is that good?"

"I would think we'll want that size for your family and my family. We won't be able to have a lot of meat with each meal, though hopefully the men will be able to get more before it's too cold to hunt."

Emma cut off one more chunk the same size as the first, and two that were about half the size. "Is that good?" she asked. She was surprised how easy it was for her to handle raw meat after her mother had taught her to never touch it. Life was different here than it had been back home, but she was starting a new life today. And she couldn't be happier.

Chapter Four

Emma headed home an hour before supper time. She wanted to make certain she could make something delicious, but she did take some of the bread Henri had made that morning to complete her meal. As someone who had grown up with little bread, she was surprised at how very much it added to a meal.

As soon as she was in her new cabin, she looked around at the room. There was little there. There were shelves along the walls on either side of the fireplace, and she had no idea why her pa and Roy hadn't added something like that. It made things so much easier.

She set the bread on the table, because they would eat it for supper, and she put her share of the butter they'd made that afternoon beside it. It would mean at least one portion of the meal was good.

She went to her hope chest and pulled out the dishes and pots and pans she'd brought with her from Iowa. Emma had no idea when they left home that she would marry so quickly, and her pa had tried to get her to leave her hope chest, but she'd dug in her heels. Now she was so thankful she had it with her.

Then she took some of the jerky her ma had provided, and she carefully followed Henri's directions for making it into a thick, meat-filled gravy. After she'd gotten it boiling, she wanted to kick herself. She should have started the rice first because it took so much longer.

Cooking definitely wasn't second nature to her as it was to Henri, but hopefully it would be soon.

Thankfully, Jared was a little later than expected, and the rice was finished before he walked in the door, looking exhausted from his day of work. He walked to her and wrapped his arms around her from behind, his whole body pressed up against her back.

"Hello," she whispered, leaning back a little. She wanted to feel him up against her front, but they had to eat first. She didn't want the food ruined.

"I'm hungry." For both the food and for her. He couldn't believe he'd waited so long to have her as his wife, and the day had finally arrived.

She laughed softly. "If you're anything like my brother, you're always hungry. Go sit down, and I'll get supper on the table."

"What did you make?" he asked.

"I'm still learning, so I made something very simple. I hope that's all right."

"Of course, it is," Jared turned her in his arms to kiss her. "I don't expect you to cook as well as my sister after less than a week of learning."

"That's a very good thing," Emma said, her arms around his neck. "We need to eat before we can get onto more interesting things."

"Like?"

She smiled, and she was certain it was a wicked-looking smile. "Going to bed early."

"Just what I was thinking."

"Then sit down, so I can feed you!"

She put the food on the table in two bowls. Having set the table while the rice was cooking, all she had to do was sit down. She reached out and took his hand in hers for their prayer.

He immediately bowed his head and prayed for the wonderful meal in front of him. When he lifted his head, he took a generous helping of the rice, and poured gravy over it. "Would you mind passing me a piece of that bread?"

Emma grabbed the bread and sliced off two pieces, spreading the fresh butter over both. She'd expected to keep one for herself, but he took both, so she sliced off another piece for her. The bread had been baked in a skillet, so it was rather flat and round, but it worked because it was delicious.

She looked at him as she took her first bite, and realized his meal was already half gone. She certainly hoped she'd cooked enough for them.

Taking her first bite, she realized the food was good, and she sighed with relief. Maybe it wasn't as good as Henri's yet, but she sure liked it.

"You did a great job on supper," Jared said as he spooned another huge helping onto his plate. "Did Henri help at all?"

"She made the bread this morning, but other than that, it was all me. Well, and my mother's jerky."

"It all tastes great. Who knew you were such a good cook?"

She laughed. "I sure wasn't a week ago. Now that I've tasted the difference, I'll always be glad Henri was so willing to teach me."

"Me too," he said, grinning at her.

"I'm a better seamstress than Henri," she said. Maybe it wasn't the time, but she needed him to know she wasn't completely inept at being a wife. She just hadn't learned to cook yet.

"Good. She always messed up when she made shirts. She and Ma both hated to have to do tedious sewing work. They loved to cook and clean and do other wifely things, but sewing was not something they were fond of. You could always tell when I tore a shirt that they were disappointed it would need to be mended."

"Really? I could make a business sewing shirts. I love to sit with a needle in my hand and just sew all day. But I have a feeling you'll want to eat often. Three times a day maybe?"

He laughed. "Yes, it would be nice if you didn't mind feeding me. I'll probably do lunch with my pa and brothers though. Then we can just eat whatever was made the night before."

She titled her head to one side. "Are they going to expect Henri and me to provide meals every night?"

"Probably. You should work it out with Henri. She did make sure we all knew how to make one breakfast and one supper, just in case we had to feed ourselves, but the truth is, none of us have enough energy to cook at night after a long day of work."

"What did you do today?" she asked, very curious.

"We're still working on finishing up the barn. It's a log barn, and it looks quite odd to be truthful, but it works." He nodded to the other end of the table. "Would you mind buttering another piece of bread for me?"

"Not at all. One or two?"

"Two."

"When do you think the barn will be ready for winter?" she asked.

"By the end of the week. We're going to have to put the horses in with the cattle for the winter, but hopefully they won't fight too much." His grin told her he was joking.

"That wouldn't be good. What will you feed them through the winter?"

"We have sacks of dried corn we brought from home. By the time we got here, the grass was too wet to make hay with it, so we won't be able to use that. On any days that it's nice out, we'll let them roam. And we'll pray. A lot. We don't have a huge herd, but we have a bull and a couple dozen heifers. It doesn't sound like much, and it's not, but it's enough to get us started. Bastian tried to convince us we should shoot one of the heifers, and we almost lost our minds. I don't know what that brother of mine is thinking!"

"I wonder if it would be possible to have some buffalo as well. Their meat is amazing, as we all know. And they're bigger, so you get more meat from each one."

He grinned. "We've talked about sectioning off a bit of land in the spring to do that. I've heard it's difficult, but it would be good to have another source of income for a while if we could make it work."

"I think that's really smart."

When he finished his third plate of food, he sat back in his chair and patted his stomach. "That was delicious, Emma."

The compliment made her feel as if she'd just brought in one of the buffalo he wanted all on her own. "I'm so glad you liked it! I'm going to get the dishes done, so we can get onto the fun part of our evening."

"You're not even a little bit shy about what we're going to do, are you?"

Emma shrugged. "Not really. Do you want me to be?"

Jared laughed softly. "Not particularly. I'm just a little surprised you seem to be looking forward to it as much as I am."

"I'm excited more than anything." She made short work of the dishes, so she could take part in what she hoped would be the most wonderful night of her life.

"Henri was really nervous."

"I got that impression. I tried to talk to her about it once, knowing I would be married soon, and I wanted to know what she thought of it, but she blushed and changed the subject. My ma was always really open with us about what it was like to be with a man, and she makes it sound like she'd rather do that than sew. And if it's that much fun, I'm ready to get on with that portion of our wedding day."

"I was expecting a blushing little bride who wouldn't want me to see her even in her nightgown."

Emma laughed. "That is not what you're getting at all. I wouldn't even bother with a nightgown, but the one Ma made me for our wedding night is so beautiful I have to wear it for at least a minute. Just so you can take it off me."

He chuckled. "I'll happily do that."

She put the last of the dishes on the shelves and turned to him. "All right. You need to go for about ten minutes so I can get that gown on."

"Are you sure I can't just watch you change into it?" He wouldn't mind that a bit.

"I'm positive. Now go walk, and I'll be ready for you when you get back."

Jared wasn't sure what to think about his bride who didn't have any worries about her wedding night. He walked to her and kissed her deeply. "Make it five minutes."

She laughed. "I hope you know we're taking it slow and easy tonight. I expect to kiss every inch of your body before you make love to me."

Jared's eyes widened. "That sounds good to me. And we'll be making love with each other." With that, he closed the door and walked out to the barn. Why he went there, he didn't know, but it seemed to make more sense to him than standing out in the cold.

The horses were there, and he gave each a pat on the nose. There were four, one each for his brothers, pa, and himself. They hadn't moved the herd in quite yet, hoping they would be able to eat the grass still on the ground for as long as possible before they had to switch to feeding them corn.

With one last pet on his favorite horse's nose, he walked slowly back to the cabin. It felt like it had been at least a half hour since he left, but he knew it was probably between five and ten minutes. Never in his life had he dreamed he would find a bride who was as eager for lovemaking as he was.

When he opened the door, he saw the lanterns had been turned down, but there was a candle lit on the chest she'd brought with her that day. It was in a corner on the far side of the bed, but it gave out enough light that he could see her.

He pushed his suspenders down each arm, as his eyes looked for her, and finally he saw her standing on the other side of the bed. His eyes widened when he realized that the top of her nightgown was only lace. He could see right through it to her small pink nipples.

As he walked toward her, his hands were at the collar of his shirt, and he unbuttoned the top button. She walked toward him and swatted his hands away. "I believe that's my job."

"Is it now?" Jared was surprised by his little bride more than he could say. He dropped his hands to his sides and stood there quietly while she went to work on the buttons of his shirt. "May I just say how much I love your nightgown, and I hope you'll wear it every night for the rest of our lives?"

Emma grinned. "Ma gave it to me at lunch today, and I was so excited!" She didn't mention that Ma had made one for Henri as well because she didn't need him thinking of his sister just then.

He reached out and caught one of her nipples between his thumb and forefinger, rolling it. "It makes me see much of what I want to see."

She sucked in a breath as he caught her nipple. "Now, I like that!"

He chuckled. "I can see you're going to enjoy this night as much as I can."

"I sure hope so! Ma said it might hurt the first time, but I should just remember how much pleasure there is to be had in our marriage bed."

His eyes widened. "She really told you that?" He knew his mother would never have said anything like that to Henri. As soon as the thought crossed his mind, he shook his head. He didn't want to think about family, not with his beautiful wife in front of him undressing him.

Emma laughed. "Ma said that too many mothers tell their daughters that they should just close their eyes and think of something else while their husband was inside them. She told me to never be that way because there was too much pleasure that I would miss out on. With as hard as life in the west will be on women, I love to know that there will be pleasure in your arms." She finished unbuttoning his shirt and pushed it off his shoulders and let it drop on the floor.

Her fingers immediately found his nipple, and she rolled it the same way he had hers. She watched his face and saw he enjoyed it just as much as she did. "Emma, if you're this aggressive the whole time, it might be over too quickly."

"Then we'll just have to try again, won't we?" She stood on her tiptoes and kissed him, wanting to feel every moment of pleasure that was available to her.

"I think you're overdressed," he said. "My shirt is gone, but you're still covered—after a fashion."

"I'm afraid this nightgown was made to get into easily, but I just can't take it off myself."

His laughter surprised him. "You're going to make this fun, aren't you?" Jared knew he'd chosen well when they shared their first kiss, but this? He didn't care if she couldn't cook. He'd eat burnt meals three times a day if she was this excited with their lovemaking.

Her smile transformed her face from simply pretty to beautiful. "I sure hope so."

He kissed her, then left a trail of kisses from her mouth to her shoulder, where a slim strap was holding her nightdress in place. He slowly lowered the strap, and his lips moved to the same place where he'd touched her through her nightgown.

He drew her nipple into his mouth and suckled softly at her breast. As she looked down at him, she felt a flood of heat going to her core. Her knees felt week, and she understood then why this was done in bed. She didn't have the strength to stand.

Her moan was loud and surprised her, but it just seemed to make him more intent on suckling. She backed toward the bed, and he followed. "I think I'm going to end up on the floor if we keep standing."

He chuckled but followed her down onto the bed. "We didn't finish the undressing portion of our fun?"

"I suppose that's going to have to happen in bed then."

"A challenge. I like challenges." He peeled the strap on her other side down, not being nearly as attentive this time. All he wanted was to see his beautiful wife without her nightgown. It had shown him a lot, but not nearly enough.

She lifted her hips as he pulled the gown down over them, and then he knelt on the bed, and just stared at her in all her glory. "I have never seen anything as beautiful as you look right now in my entire life."

"Well, take your pants off then. I want to see too!"

He was positive she shouldn't be saying anything like that, but what did it matter? It was only the two of them, and he may want a lady during the day, but he wanted a lover at night, and as far as he was concerned there was nothing they couldn't say or do together.

He stood beside the bed, surprised at how weak his own knees were. Unbuttoning his pants, he let them fall to his feet, even as he pushed his underwear down. He knew his member stood at attention, and he was a bit worried it would scare her, but she smiled as if he'd just given her a present.

As soon as he was back on the bed and once again kneeling beside her, she took him in her hand, stroking his flesh softly. "I don't think that's a good idea!" he told her.

"Oh, but it's so soft. I think I like it."

He closed his eyes, and just let her touch. She was in no hurry for this night to end, so if he lost his control now, he had a feeling there would be no problem returning to his state.

Chapter Five

Emma abruptly let go and pulled Jared down beside her, kissing him with all she was worth. "Slow and steady wins the race..." she said softly.

He was shocked at all she seemed to know about how a man's body worked, but he was starting to believe every woman should enter their marriage with the knowledge this slip of a girl had in her head.

When his hands moved to explore her down between her legs, she arched her hips and moaned softly. She didn't seem to mind when he moved his fingers along her core and even moved one inside her.

She clutched at his shoulders, and pulled his head down to her, kissing him instead. "That feels so strange and good and strange all at once."

"Strange and you want me to stop? Or strange and you want me to keep going?" Jared worried he was moving too fast for her, but he'd expected the whole thing to last ten minutes, and it certainly wasn't working out that way.

"More please!"

He chuckled. "How about I replace my fingers with something else?"

"Not yet," she said. "Just a little more playing with each other."

He groaned. "You're killing me! I'm not sure how much longer I can last..."

"Think of how good it will feel when it's time!" Emma moved her hands to his broad shoulders. She'd noticed them before she'd even noticed his face and touching them...well it brought her joy. Her hands moved all over his back and down to his bottom, which she cupped in her hands. "I like touching you."

His mouth met hers in another kiss, this one more deeply passionate than ever before. It felt as if he was trying to imitate what he would be doing to her body in just a bit.

His fingers were still inside her, and she felt pressure building in her as well, but she didn't want his fingers in her when she experienced the miracle her mother had told her would happen.

She moved his hand away, and very hoarsely said, "Now would be good."

Jared didn't have to be told twice. He covered her body with his own and moved into her as slowly as he could possibly manage.

When she gasped and arched into him, his eyes widened, and he began moving within her.

She wrapped her legs around his waist to feel him even deeper within her. There was a little pain, but she knew what was coming, and she wanted it desperately.

She felt herself rising ever higher, and she arched her entire body when the miracle happened.

As soon as he saw she'd reached her pleasure, he moved faster, and only cared about his own pleasure. He finished quickly, and moved to her side, afraid of crushing her.

"I liked feeling you on top of me," she protested.

"You're going to be the death of me, Emma Appleby."

She smiled with pleasure at her new name. "I like the sound of that. My new name."

Pulling her to him, he wasn't even a little bit surprised when she threw her leg over him and snuggled even closer. "Our wedding night was so much more than I thought it could possibly be. Thank you for that."

She made a little humming sound in her throat. "Just wait until I figure out what I'm doing." She was content to lay there as close to him as she possibly could, knowing his seed was inside her, and she could already be expecting his baby. Of course, she'd rather put off childbirth for a little while. She wanted to have plenty of time for the two of them to have fun before babies came along.

EMMA WOKE BEFORE THE sun was up the following morning, and she was surprised by the deep ache between her legs. It would remind her all day what the two of them had enjoyed together and make her excited for it to happen again that evening. She was going to like being married very much!

She dressed quickly in the cold morning air and immediately went to start the fire. Then she went to the stove and whipped up some pancakes with eggs her mother had given her. It was a meal she'd never made alone, but she hoped she did well with it. She wanted to save what little bacon was left for Sunday mornings, which she thought should always be a good meal.

Emma heard Jared stirring just as she flipped the first four pancakes onto a plate. "If you want, you can get started on these while I make more. Then you can eat your fill while they're hot, and you can let me know when you're done."

She was surprised to see that Jared was walking toward her instead of getting dressed. He grabbed her kissing her. "I was disappointed to realize you were already awake. I hoped to wake you up by making love to you again."

"That sounds lovely. I'll wait for you tomorrow."

"You could wake me up the same way."

The tingling between her legs started again. "Perhaps we should eat breakfast and then visit the bed once more."

Jared smiled. "We'll make sure to do that." Instead of going back to dress, he took the plate from her, added a bit of butter, and the syrup on one shelf, and sat down at the table to eat.

She didn't know why, but that made her blush. All they'd done the night before didn't bother her a single bit but seeing him sit at their table completely naked made her feel embarrassed. "Don't you think you should put some clothes on?"

"Why? If we're going to go back to bed after breakfast, it feels as if it's wasting time." Jared cut into his pancakes. "We'll pray after the meal this morning."

After his eighth pancake, he said, "I think I'm finished."

"All right." She flipped the last four pancakes onto her plate and moved to sit with him at the table. "We can pray now."

He bowed his head and thanked God for their meal and the miracle that was his bride. She was touched by his words.

"I'm not a miracle. I couldn't even cook a week ago."

"But now you know how to make several different meals. And I'm not talking about your cooking when I call you a miracle."

She grinned. "I cannot express how much I enjoyed last night. I wish there was time for us to lock ourselves in this cabin and just spend our days lolling about in bed."

"I never thought I'd pray for a blizzard, but I think it's about to happen," he told her, picking up her hand and kissing the palm.

She giggled. "I think you need to have the barn done first, and if we could have just a bit more meat set aside."

"Stop being logical when I want to make love with you!"

"Let me eat a little breakfast first…" She moved her foot to his shin, stroking it with the side of her foot.

He groaned. "Eat fast."

"You're always in such a hurry. Don't you want to take time to smell the roses?"

He shook his head. "I really don't."

"Will you be working on the barn again today?" she asked between bites. And she was eating much faster than she knew was healthful, but despite her teasing, she was feeling a bit anxious for their endeavors as well.

He nodded. "Until it's done. Then we'll hunt as much as we can every day, so we'll have meat for the winter."

"I know my brother is planning to share anything he hunts with us and your family."

Jared shrugged. "We'll take him up on it, but it will be nice to not have to worry about meat all winter. Your ma makes wonderful jerky."

"She does." It wasn't as good as Henri's, but she wasn't going to say that aloud. She would sound envious, and she didn't want to, but she knew she was, deep inside.

"That will help a lot. Did you learn to salt meat yesterday?" he asked.

"I did, but I'm going back to do more with them today. Next week we'll start alternating who is teaching whom. Henri wants to get better at sewing, and the ladies in my family want to all learn how to cook better."

"You womenfolk make me feel like we should be inviting your brother and pa to work with us, but I'm not sure how that would work."

She shook her head. "No, you keep doing as you're doing. We ladies will work together." She got to her feet and pulled her dress and petticoat over her head. There was no point in being shy after last night, though she hadn't felt terribly shy then either.

"You're done eating?" he asked.

When she nodded, he pulled her toward the bed. What a way to start the day.

AFTER FINISHING THE breakfast dishes later that morning, Emma wandered down the hill to Henri's cabin. Jared had promised to bring down all the jars he and his brothers had brought west so they could do more salting of the meat.

When she arrived at Henri's she saw there was a moose hanging from a tree as well. Until that day, Emma hadn't realized just what a good hunter her brother was.

She was the first one at Henri's, and Roy was just leaving for the morning. "Jared will be bringing all the jars he and his brother brought west. Then we'll have the supplies we need to finish up the salting."

"If we run out, there are other ways, but I prefer the use of jars." Henri kissed Roy goodbye, blushing. "Will you be home for lunch?"

Roy shook his head. "No, Pa and I will just have some jerky and keep working while the work is good."

"We got a light dusting of snow last night," Emma said, grinning. "I love snow."

Roy left, putting on his boots outside the house. Emma could hear him stomping into them.

Henri nodded but looked a bit worried. "I'm just a little frightened we won't be able to get enough meat in before winter is truly upon us. I know they'll still bundle up and go out, but it's safer for them now."

Emma nodded. "It is. I shouldn't be excited for snow."

"But you are, and that's all right." Henri did the breakfast dishes with Emma's help. "When is Jared supposed to come with those jars?"

"He said he was gathering them and bringing them down first thing." Emma heard a wagon pull up in front of the cabin. "And there he is."

Jared had brought Sam to help him carry the jars inside. Henri hurried to the door to open it for them.

Emma watched Jared walk into the cabin with two crates of the jars, which he deposited on the table. He ignored his siblings, and walked over to her, whispering in her ear, "I already miss you."

"You're not alone in that," she whispered back, wishing they really could spend the whole day in the cabin, whether it was proper or not.

Sam shook his head at the two of them. "You'd think you two just got married or something."

Henri hurried outside mumbling something about fetching water to boil the jars.

"Now look!" Sam said. "You scared Henri away." He walked back out to the wagon, but he was shaking his head.

Emma giggled. "We need to get Sam married off, so he'll stop making fun of us."

"But then he won't have a place to be alone with his bride?" Jared grinned. "Come to think of it, it would be fun to see Sam tortured that way."

"You're mean," she said, shaking her head. "Bring the jars in and go away. I can't work with you here. I'd be too busy thinking about how good you feel inside me."

"You just keep thinking that. We'll be alone again this evening."

"Yes, we will!" Emma said grinning at him.

"Okay, works for me!" Jared hurried to help his brother carry the jars into the house so they could get back to building the barn. He didn't want to ever leave Emma, but there was no choice. Duty before fun.

Emma took jars out of the crates while the men finished carrying them inside. When they were done, she said, "Thank you. I think we can take it from here." She picked up a bucket to go out and get some water from the creek. It would be so nice when the ground was soft enough they could dig a well, but for now, toting it from the creek worked.

Jared frowned. "Where are you taking that bucket?"

"We're going to need a lot of water to wash this many jars, so I'll get a bucket full of water from the creek."

He shook his head. "I'll do it."

"But Henri is doing the same thing. Why can't I?"

"Because you're my wife. I don't think Henri should be doing it either. Come on, Sam. One more job before we get back to the real work."

"I can do it!" Emma said, feeling like she was being coddled, which didn't please her a great deal.

"You can, but you shouldn't have to." Jared took her bucket and he and Sam headed off toward the creek.

Emma shook her head. Apparently, Jared had no idea how strong she was. She'd have to show him what she could do. It had never mattered before that she was capable of a great many things. Now it suddenly was.

While Emma waited for the buckets to come back, she unpacked the jars, and added another piece of the wood to stoke the fire. She wasn't going to sit around and laze the day away when she could be doing something useful.

Henri came back before her brothers, shaking her head. "Pa used to get on those boys all the time when they wouldn't fetch water for my ma and me. And there they are now, refusing to let us do it. What is wrong with them? I swear, my brothers have rocks for brains."

Henri looked at the jars that were taken out and smiled when she could see the fire had been stoked. "Do you know if your sisters are coming today to help us with the salting?"

"I believe so. I haven't heard anything different."

"Good. Many hands make for light work. And I happen to know your brother is hunting again today, so I expect this will be our task all week. I'll teach you to cook something new for lunch, though."

"All right. I think that sounds fine, and then I can make that something new for Jared for our supper."

"Oh, I was going to teach you to make johnny cakes, and he only wants to eat them for breakfast. We'll make a soup with some of the meat, and then we won't have to salt it. We'll make enough for supper for Roy and me, and if you want to have a fire outside, we can work on them together."

"That sounds good. I've always wanted to know how to make a good hearty soup."

"You'll know before lunch time." Henri frowned. "I do wish Ma had agreed to bring barley. I love it in soup, but Ma said the room should be used for more important things."

"I've never had it."

Henri put as many jars as could fit into her cast iron pot, and then she added water until each jar was covered. She hung the pot over the fire and turned back to Emma. "When I make a soup, I make sure that I use a meat, which I make the broth from, either potatoes or rice or barley, and some vegetables. I mix and match with what I have on hand, making each soup a little different from the last, but all are equally good."

"The same way you serve jerky and gravy over rice or potatoes?"

"Yes! As we get finished processing the meat, we'll have time for me to make noodles, and I sometimes use those instead of rice or barley. I like to have a selection of different things, so no one gets tired of soup. Each one is a little different. My favorite soup is barley, with chunks of beef cut up, and little pieces of carrot. I could eat that for every meal! My brothers tend to get sick of it, though. They like as much variety as we can give them."

Emma nodded. "I can't wait to see how you make your broth. I think I understand the rest of the process. What seasonings do you use?"

"Salt, of course. Pepper if I have it. I like to use garlic as well, but that will be scarcer here." Henri sighed. "I think we live in a beautiful place, but I sure do wish we had some more spices to cook with."

"I can understand that. This will be fun!"

"We'll have to hurry with the jars so we will have time to make the soup." Henri bit her lip. "Let's make another trip to the creek for water, and then we'll be ready to boil the next batch. I think we should do two batches today."

Emma picked up one of the buckets the men had brought back, and they walked toward the creek together. The wind was blowing much harder that day, and Emma wished she'd brought her scarf and mittens. Or a hat. She'd always hated wearing hats, but it would keep her head warm as they walked to the creek and back.

Chapter Six

When Henri and Emma returned from the creek, Abigail and Barbara were there waiting for them. "Where did you go?" Barbara asked.

"We had to get water to boil the jars to sanitize them," Emma explained. The previous pot of water had boiled, and Henri took each jar out with a pair of tongs.

They quickly refilled the dutch oven and put it back over the stove. "Now we need one more trip to the creek to get more water."

Abigail looked at Barbara. "We'll go. You've both already been out, and it's chilly."

Emma thought about arguing, but her sister was right. It was their turn to go out in the cold.

After they'd left, she and Henri went out to cut off meat for their soup for later. "We should make the girls cut off the roasts when they get back," Emma said. "Ma taught us all to be afraid to touch raw meat, and they need to get past that if they want to be good cooks."

Henri nodded. "I think that's a great idea." Heading back to the house with all the meat on a board, Emma became curious.

"Why didn't you have Roy add shelves in here? It would be so much easier for you to store things."

"I have requested it, but I asked he wait until winter, when he won't spend so much time hunting. That's something he can do while we're trapped inside in a blizzard."

Emma smiled, because the mention of a blizzard reminded her that Jared had told her he was praying for blizzards. "Something funny?" Henri asked.

"Just something Jared said this morning. Nothing important." Emma wasn't about to share that with someone who was easily embarrassed by sexual matters.

"So, to make the broth, I cut the meat into chunks, and cook them for an hour or two over a fire. I tend to put the vegetables in as well because it helps flavor the broth nicely, and always some salt and pepper."

Emma nodded. "Would an onion be good for broth?"

"Yes. I hate that we don't have any. You would peel off the paper type substance on the outside of the onion and chop it into small pieces. They would stay in and flavor the soup." Henri grinned. "You're getting good at knowing which flavors to put together." She cut the meat in front of her into small squares for the soup and noticed Emma was already following along. "You are going to be one of the best cooks around!"

"I don't know about that, but I am enjoying learning. It makes me so happy when Jared is fond of one of my meals. He told me supper last night was delicious." Emma smiled as she cut up the meat the same way Henri was doing.

"That's wonderful. I think you're a very natural cook. You only needed to learn a few things about what to do so you could get started."

"Thank you for teaching me those things."

"Happy to do it. Then you can take half the cooking for my family off your plate."

Emma sighed. "I had a feeling it was going to come to that."

"Of course, it is. I can't let them try to fend for themselves when I know how horrible they are at cooking."

"I know. I'll help how I can, but would you keep making the bread for now? I'm intimidated by it."

Henri laughed. "It is one of the harder things to learn over an open fire. We had a beautiful oven at home, and I miss it terribly. As soon as we get all the meat put up, we're going to have a day where we do nothing but bake bread and cinnamon rolls. With as many as are in our two families, it'll all get eaten."

"That is very true."

"Oh, that's something else my ma taught me! If there's ever bread left over, and it does happen rarely, she would hollow out the bread and make bowls out of it, and she would serve soup in them. You can get two bowls from each loaf of bread. When it's shaped like real bread, of course."

Emma nodded, understanding exactly what Henri was saying. "I will keep that in mind for when I start baking loaves of bread then."

By the time they'd cut up the meat, Emma's sisters were back with more water. They pulled the Dutch oven from the fireplace and again removed the jars, and then they filled it with all of the meat Henri had cut up, and Emma took the extra Dutch oven outside, starting a fire, and then putting the oven in the fire. She added the meat and one of the buckets of water before going in to chop up vegetables with Henri.

While the soup cooked, they taught the girls how to cut the meat off the carcasses to be processed. Barbara squealed when the blood touched her hand which was very predictable behavior for her, but Abigail did as she was told with no fuss.

They packed the salt around the meat and put it into the freshly cleaned jars. They had a dozen done by the time the rice in the broth had cooked enough to eat it.

Emma and Abigail ate her soup, and Henri and Barbara ate the soup Henri had made. That way they would both still have enough food for their suppers. "Do you have bread left from yesterday?" Henri asked as they finished up their lunch.

"I do have one loaf left. Should we really call them loaves when they look more like pancakes?" Emma asked.

"One should be enough with the soup. And yes, we're calling them loaves, because I will soon be making bread in its correct shape again. You have no idea how much it bothers me to make flat bread."

Emma laughed and shook her head. "You have no idea how much it would please me to *be able* to make your flat bread."

Henri smiled and nodded. "We both have our strengths, and soon, we should have each other's strengths."

Emma thought it was odd that they'd been married only a week apart, but it seemed as if Henri had been married for much longer. She just seemed so sure of herself as a wife.

By the time Emma left that afternoon, the soup she'd made in hand, she was ready to be home with just her own thoughts for a little while. She walked up the hill as leisurely as she could, considering how steep it was.

When she walked into the cabin she shared with Jared, she let out a sigh of relief. An hour or two alone would do wonders for her.

She built a small fire and hung the soup over it. It was done, but Henri had told her it wouldn't hurt to keep it on a small fire, and it would stay warm that way. The difference in the way Henri did things and the way her ma did things was truly amazing to her.

While waiting for Jared to get home, she swept the entire cabin, made up the bed, and hurried to dust everything. The cabin was mostly spotless, but she certainly wanted to keep it that way. She'd have some of the meat when she left Henri's the next day, and she knew it would make her feel as if she knew more about what she was doing.

When the cabin was truly as clean as she liked it, she sat down at the table, and worked on a small gift for Henri, to thank her for all she'd done to help her. It was a small gown for a baby, and she was adorning it with lace she'd tatted herself.

She loved the idea of being an aunt, but she really didn't feel ready to be a mother yet. She and Jared hadn't had enough time to just be a married couple, and they needed that before the demands of a baby came into play. She wanted children, yes, but it wasn't a driving force in her life.

The little gown was mostly finished when she set it down to set the table so supper would be ready as soon as Jared walked in the door.

She was surprised to hear him a little before expected, but Emma wasn't about to complain. Any extra time spent with Jared was wonderful in her book.

Emma had finished putting the bowls of soup on the table and cut several pieces of bread when Jared made it into the house. "I hope you're hungry!" Emma called.

Jared grinned, walking to her in his sock feet. Someone must have trained him well not to track mud into the house. She wasn't sure if that should be a rule when the floor was part mud, but she certainly wasn't going to complain. When she finally had a real house for her family, it would be a good habit for him to be in.

"I thought of you all day," he said, his lips at her neck.

"I thought of you as well! I'm glad that no matter what we do during the day, we'll have each other in the evenings."

"Yes!" He looked at the table. "Soup tonight?"

She nodded. "Your sister taught me to make several different kinds of soup today."

"I wish we'd thought to bring barley with us," Jared said. "My favorite soups all have barley."

"I have never enjoyed barley, but I think we both know that could be because of how my mother made it. She usually just fried it up for us to eat."

Jared made a face. "Ma and Henri always use it in soup. I cannot imagine frying it. Wouldn't that make it hard?"

"It does!" Emma agreed. She moved to her chair at the table and took a seat.

Jared sat as well, reaching for her hand as he prayed.

"How's the barn coming?" Emma asked.

"It's going to be another few days before it's done. Pa insists we have a separate area for the heifers who need to be milked. He says it will save time, but it sure doesn't feel like a time saver right now."

"I can see his reasoning. Oh, Ma told me Sunday that she'll be giving us some of her hens and one rooster. She brought too much for one family."

He frowned. "So now we need a chicken enclosure, or another small room in the barn for the chickens." He rubbed the back of his neck. "I feel like we're spending so much time building structures that there will be no time to hunt for the meat we're going to need."

"You know my family is sharing all their meat with us, right?"

Jared nodded. "I just hate that we need so much help right now. I believe a man should supply what his family needs, not his wife's family." He sighed. "I'll accept the help, of course, because we'll need it, but I would prefer to find a way to do for us myself."

"I just don't think that could be possible for anyone who has just arrived on the trail. Very few people knew what all they should bring. Ma had the chickens trained, and they never wandered off. We lost one chicken along the way when it was injured, so Ma just made chicken and rice that evening."

He shook his head. "Your ma thought ahead more than I did. I should have thought about needing eggs along the way and when we got here."

"No one could bring everything they thought they needed. I just pray we'll be able to get what we need here." The area was remote, with only Indians and one trader close. The things they'd considered necessities at home, may not be available there.

"I don't think we need much besides each other," he said, his voice deep.

She glanced up from her soup and saw the now-familiar look in his eyes. "After the dishes," she told him. But her body was heating up already. Her ma had been right. She loved being with Jared.

"How about before the dishes and then after the dishes."

She laughed. "Work before play. It's how I was raised, and I'm sure you were raised the same way."

"I was. I've never really wanted to break that rule before now though."

She smiled. "Work first. Play later." It was hard for her to stick to the rule she'd always been taught as well, but he could wait. It only took her a few minutes to wash, wipe, and put the dishes away.

He continued to steadily eat his soup. "This is very good," he finally said. She could tell he was disappointed, but they both knew the correct way to do things.

"Thank you," she said softly.

"Is there anything else you absolutely need here? I'm willing to make whatever I can to make your life easier."

Emma shook her head. "I'm doing most of my work at Henri's anyway. I know that will probably change when winter hits, but I'll do what needs to be done."

"You're sure?"

She nodded emphatically. "I have all I need."

"Let me know if that changes."

While he ate his third bowl of soup, Emma started on the dishes. When he finished his last bite, he brought her the dish and spoon, as well as his coffee cup to wash. "Do I need to go for a walk again tonight?" he asked.

She shook her head. "Not at all. If you want to, go, but I only wanted you to leave last night so I could put on the nightgown my mother made."

"You don't need to wear a nightgown tonight. You know I'm just going to take it off you if you do."

"I'm fully aware."

When the last dish was wiped and put up on the shelf where it belonged, he took her hand and walked to the bed. "You undress, and I'll get the lanterns."

She nodded. "All right."

He had a predatory look on his face as he approached her, and she couldn't help but smile. Now they could take the time to do whatever they wanted to do. Being married was the best thing that had ever happened to her.

BY THE END OF THE WEEK, Emma felt better about baking bread, and she was able to attempt to make her own bread on Saturday, when she stayed home instead of heading down the hill to Henri's house.

She felt a bit daring, so when the bread was finished, she made a cake as well. She carefully frosted it just as Henri had taught her and left it on one end of the table for dessert that evening.

For supper, she decided to get a bit creative, so she cut the elk meat she had for supper that night into tiny chunks. She cooked them, using the juices from the meat to form a gravy, and then she put a pot of rice on. When she mixed it all together at the end of the day, she took a small taste, realizing that it was delicious. She knew she was already a far better cook than her mother ever had been or would be.

When Jared arrived home that evening from working on the barn, he stood in the doorway for a moment with a big grin on his face. "We added one more small room to the barn. It has roosts for chickens."

Emma's face lit up with excitement. "I can get them from Ma tomorrow or Monday then!"

He nodded. "And the barn is finished. Now it's just a matter of hunting until we can't hunt anymore."

"Oh, that's exciting! What's your favorite game?"

He shrugged. "I like rabbits a lot, but I don't think it would be wise to hunt for them. There's too little meat on them."

"That's true," she said. "What about the bigger game?"

"No one I know agrees with me on this, but I love bear meat. If I could get a bear before they go into hibernation for the winter, we would be set for meat for the entire winter."

Emma shrugged. "I haven't had bear that was cooked well. I don't know if I'll enjoy it or not."

"I guess we'll find out. I'm not sure we can let our personal tastes matter too much anyway," he said as he took off his coat and hung his hat on a peg. "I think we're going to have to eat whatever is available if we don't want to starve this winter. Next year we'll be a great deal more prepared."

"Yes, we will! Hopefully, we'll even have some chicken to eat. Chicken is my very favorite meat, but it's not worth it to kill the chickens that will be the start of our flock."

He moved to sit at the table. He was early, so he hadn't expected supper to be ready. "I like chicken. Of all the meats, I like beef though. I think that's why I like the idea of being a rancher so much."

"I can understand that. Beef is good. Your sister told me about a beef and barley soup with little carrots she and your ma used to make. I want to get my hands on some barley so I can try to replicate it."

When she carried their plates of food to the table, she set his in front of him. "I made something new today. Henri didn't teach me to make this, so if it's awful, you can only blame me. She keeps telling me cooking is creative, and I need to combine things that sound good together, and that's what I did."

Jared looked down at the food on his place. "This looks really good."

"I sure hope it is." Emma knew she thought it was, but she didn't really have a feel for things he would like yet.

After their prayer, he ate one bite and nodded emphatically. "Absolutely delicious. I knew it wouldn't take Henri long to get you to be a wonderful cook. I almost don't think you need any more lessons."

Emma laughed. "I need more receipts is what I need. I should ask for receipts when we go to the quilting circle at the church next week."

"I think that's a great idea!"

Chapter Seven

On Sunday, they attended church, listening to a wonderful sermon by Pastor Scott on loving thy neighbor. "Especially in these times, we all need to reach out and help each other. This will be a winter that is almost as hard as it was on the trail, if not harder. So, look around you at all the people who helped you and whom you've helped in the past, and think about who could use a small blessing. Is there only one man and five children? Help him finish his shelter for the winter. Is there a woman who was left a widow along the trail? Take her some meat so she and her children don't starve. I know all of you know how to help one another, but you're focused on getting yourself ready for winter, and not worried about the people around you. If you can donate in any way to some of these families, time, food, whatever it is that you can help with, I implore you to do so."

Emma's thoughts were on the sermon as they drove home. She kept thinking about who she could serve. "I think it's time for me to be involved in making meals for your family," she said softly. "Henri is wonderful and always willing to help, but she can't do it all on her own."

Jared nodded. "I'm going to share any of the game I get with some of the widows...or families where the father is sick or injured. We can do so much as a community, and I think the pastor's right. We should all be doing all we can for others."

Emma thought for a moment. "I have a lot of fabric scraps. I could perhaps make a rag doll or even a dress for a little girl or perhaps a gown for a new baby. All the people that we know, and love are going to need things, and we're healthy and strong. Maybe one deer for us and one for another family. However, it works out, we should share the little we have."

"Perhaps you could watch children for a few hours, so their ma can go for a walk alone. Just so she has some time to think without children running about screaming."

"All good suggestions. I'll get together with Henri and my mother and sisters. We'll figure out how we can help as many people as possible. Perhaps it's simply taking them a meal or two."

"Exactly. I'm glad we think alike on things like this." Jared looked over at his beautiful bride and saw more to her than he had. When he'd first courted her, she'd been a pretty face atop a beautiful body. Now though? He saw her for the person inside, and he felt so much more for her. A month ago, he never would have believed that his feelings for her could intensify. He would have to find a way to tell her that she was more to him than a body to relieve himself with. She was quickly becoming his everything.

"Can we stop at Henri's on the way?" Emma asked.

"Of course. Did you forget something there?"

"No, I want to let her know that I'm happy to do the meal for your family this evening. It may even be edible!"

He chuckled. "You've become a wonderful cook. I have no idea why you're so worried about your cooking now. You haven't messed up a meal in over a week to my knowledge."

"A week. Henri's probably never messed up a meal."

He shook his head. "To my knowledge she hasn't, but she had a very good teacher. And now you do as well."

She jumped from the wagon when he stopped in front of his sister's house, and he frowned. "You're supposed to wait for my help."

Emma laughed and shook her head. "I've not needed help getting down from a wagon for many years. We'll be formal at times, but I can do things to take care of myself as well."

She hurried to the door and knocked. Normally, she wouldn't knock on Henri's door, but knowing her brother was home with her, she was a bit afraid of what she might walk in on.

Henri came to the door and opened it wide. "You should stay for lunch. Bring Jared in here with you!"

Emma shook her head. "I appreciate the offer, but I'm here to tell you I'll take care of your family for supper tonight. It'll be much easier on you if we take turns."

Henri bit her lip as if she wasn't certain if she wanted to accept the offer, but finally she nodded. "I do think that would be wonderful, if you truly don't mind."

"I don't mind at all. I was thinking about the pastor's sermon and all the ways we can help others. Perhaps we can talk about that with Ma and the girls tomorrow. Even if we just made a meal for families who don't have as much. What do you think?"

"I was thinking the same thing. It's scary because we don't know how much we'll need, but if we share, I'm certain we will be blessed for it."

"Yes. All right. Spend time with my brother, and I'll spend time with yours."

"Sounds good to me." Henri watched as her brother helped Emma into the wagon. It was funny to watch him and how gentle and caring he was with Emma. He'd certainly never behaved like she needed help with anything, and now he was doing things for Emma that he'd never dreamed of helping her with. It was good.

"Now I have to figure out what to cook," Emma said as they drove up the hill. "I could do a stew with rice. I've done that for your family before, and I think it was all right."

"It was better than all right. Stew sounds perfect, and we can have it here as well. No need to fix two meals."

"Oh good!"

"Don't you ever cook beans?" he asked.

She nodded. "I haven't discussed them with Henri, but I know my family always preferred my beans to Ma's. She never put enough water in them, and they were dry and hard."

He shook his head. "I don't know how you survived as long as you did."

"If you don't know what something should taste like, then there's no way to know if you've cooked it well."

"Yes, talk to Henri, but I think it's time to reintroduce beans and rice to our meals."

"Probably. I know we all got sick of them on the trail, but I also know there are a lot left. We'll be happy to eat them if we run out of meat."

"Eating them once a week or so will make the meat stretch further. And you can put a small amount of meat in with the beans. That's what Ma and Henri always did. We still complained, but it was good." Jared felt guilty for as much as he'd complained about all the beans on the trail.

"I'll try that. Is there a certain kind of meat?"

"I like it with just about anything. We can't be picky eaters right now."

"I'll make it happen then."

Emma made to jump out of the wagon, but he put a hand on her knee. "Wait for me."

She felt silly waiting for him to help her do something she could do perfectly well on her own. "Oh! We forgot to stop at my parents' and get our chickens."

"Do you know how many it will be?"

"Ma said we could have one rooster and four laying hens. If we give them a few months, we'll have a lot more. Lots of baby chicks in the spring. I would even hold off on collecting eggs until we know that the chicks are hatched."

"I never thought I'd be a chicken farmer."

She grinned. "I guess it's not something people think about."

Instead of helping her down, Jared walked around the wagon and climbed back up to drive to her parents' house.

When they got to the house, he helped her down and then they went to the cabin together. Her sister, Abigail, opened the door. "Ma, it's Emma and Jared!"

"Get them the chickens and rooster I set apart from the others, and then invite them to lunch," Ma called back.

"No thanks to lunch, Ma. I already know what I'm fixing!" Emma didn't really know what she was making, but she was certain whatever it was, it would taste better than what Ma was cooking.

Abigail grabbed a shawl and hurried outside to the enclosure Pa and Roy had made for the chickens. She pointed to the birds, in a small cage together, and Jared picked up the cage. "You sure you want chickens?" he asked Emma, who nodded.

"We've always had chickens. They're my favorite!"

Jared wasn't sure what to say to that. "Is one of these going to be chicken and dumplings one day?"

"I've never had that. Is it good?"

"Until you know how to make them, you will not be stopping your lessons with Henri. It's one of my favorite meals, and we'll have it as often as possible."

Emma laughed. "I'll do my best, but I can't promise to make it just like Henri does."

"I don't want you to do everything just like Henri. I have a feeling you could even make it better."

"I don't know about that..."

With the cage in the back of the wagon, they drove back up the hill for the final time that morning. This time Emma waited for him to help her down, and they carried the cage over to the barn. "I think we should take the cage back to Ma," she said after they'd let the chickens out in their own little room.

He nodded. "I'm sure she'll be sharing chickens with more people than just us."

"She shares eggs with Roy and Henri, but I think she'll give them some of her flock in the spring. I know I'd rather not ask her to take care of them, and then take her eggs, and I have a feeling Henri will feel just the same."

"I'm sure you're right. Henri likes to be self-sufficient. Did she try to argue with you taking supper to my family?" he asked.

"She did. But I told her she deserves a break, and we're going to start alternating days. Now that I've learned to bake my own bread, I'm feeling a great deal more confident about my cooking."

"What are we having for lunch today?" he asked, already getting hungry.

She thought quickly about what she had on hand. "Would you mind if I made jerky gravy and your choice of potatoes or rice for them to go on?"

"I choose rice," he said. "And that sounds wonderful. You've made it for me a couple of times now, and it's delicious. I do know there won't be a lot of variety in what we eat this winter."

"But in the spring, I can plant a kitchen garden, and we'll have fresh vegetables. I brought seed packets in my hope chest."

"That was very smart. We don't know what kind of soil we have here, but I pray it will grow everything we need."

"If it won't, I'll use some of the special fertilizer your cattle are making."

He chuckled. "You are definitely not the shy girl I expected to be married to."

"My ma told me I always had to act shy around you until there was a physical display of affection." She rolled her eyes. "So, I did my best. After you kissed me, I began to act like myself."

"Trust me, I'm not complaining. I'd rather have you than some girl who would have a fit of the vapors if she saw my bare chest."

Emma threw back her head and laughed. "That's not something that's going to happen with me at all."

"I'm so glad. I think you would have already died from vapors if you'd been that way." He gave her an exaggerated wink, and she giggled.

"I think after lunch, we need some time to just be together as a couple."

"Is clothing optional?" he asked.

"Of course not. We need our clothes off for the kind of fun I'm thinking about."

"I like the way you think, Emma. I really do."

She grinned, leaning her head against his shoulder for a moment. "Have I mentioned how happy I am that you finally asked my pa to court me?" she asked. "I've been watching your shoulders and your cute bottom since we left Independence."

For once, he looked embarrassed. "You were looking at my bottom?"

"Oh, yes. I wanted to feel it naked it my hands, but I didn't think it would be proper to walk up to you and tell you that."

He laughed. "Emma?"

"Yes, Jared?"

"My life is so much better because you're in it. You're the woman I need to spend all my life with. I don't know what I would do if I ever lost you."

"You're not going to lose me!" She shook her head. "I'm strong. You'll see."

As soon as they were inside, she went to work on their lunch, remembering to start the rice first this time.

He watched her while she cooked for a few minutes, and then he pulled out a knife and a small block of wood. He'd always enjoyed whittling, and he was certain he could make a beautiful Christmas present for her, while she did chores around the house.

It was a quiet leisurely day for them, and they felt closer as a couple by the time it was over. She also felt weak as a rag doll, but her happiness was such that she didn't care. Jared was the only person who could make her this happy.

EMMA MET UP WITH THE other women after cleaning and doing the breakfast dishes on Monday. All of them were thinking of ways they could work together to help different families in need.

"Do we have any widowers?" Henri asked. "I mean, I know my pa, but there have to be others."

"Most of them were married on the trail," Emma said. "Your pa may be the only one left. Even Mr. Bedwell got married, and we all know that was not expected."

Henri smiled. "Katie is so good for him. She is a good wife and mother to his boys. She's already expecting you know." Emma could see on Henri's face that she was eager for children in a way she simply wasn't. She would take the children God gave her and love them with everything inside her, but she hoped they were two or three years down the road.

"So, let's think about the widows then. I'm sure many of them could use some time away from their children. There are a few widows that didn't marry, I think."

"There's old Mrs. Jenkins. She's super nice, but her children are grown. She's probably lonely." Ma pursed her lips. "I think I'll go visit her with a pie or cake. Well, as long as Emma or Henri are willing to make it. The cake I tried turned out awful."

Barbara nodded. "It really did. We don't want her poisoning anyone with her cakes, so it would be best if someone else made it."

Ma frowned at Barbara, but she continued. "I will take her a few of the salted roasts, and one fresh. Then perhaps we can take her a roast from every animal shot by one of our men? It would take her a few days to eat one, so it would provide a lot of food for her."

"Do you know where she settled?" Henri asked, taking notes on a piece of paper.

"She's down near the church," Emma said. "I remember her telling me that at the church raising." Henri looked deep in thought for a moment. "I wonder if she'd like my cookies instead of a cake or pie?"

"I would love to learn to make your cookies, so let's say cookies," Emma replied.

"We'll make that a plan then. What day do you think you'll go, Mrs. Williams?"

"Perhaps on Friday. On Sunday, she sees people at church. On Wednesday, she will go to the quilting circle. So, if I go Friday, that will be something to look forward to."

"Perfect!" Henri said.

"We'll tell her you're coming on Wednesday," Emma said.

"Who next?" Henri asked.

Chapter Eight

By Wednesday, Henri and the Williams women knew who they were going to help and when. They spent the morning working with the quilting circle.

It was fun to have time to sit and chat with the others. Mary and her mother were there together, and it made Emma wonder who was caring for all of Mrs. Mitchell's other children. "You didn't bring your children?" she asked.

"They are old enough to mind themselves for a few hours," Mrs. Mitchell said. "I left them a cold lunch they can eat when they get hungry. I needed a little time on my own."

"I can understand that completely." Emma's younger siblings were there helping with the quilt they were making. "Who are we making the quilt for?"

"This first one is for the pastor and his wife," Margaret Prewitt said, speaking softly. Her children were playing quietly at her feet, and she was very noticeably pregnant with her third, who was her husband Jamie's first.

"I think the first should go to them. We can't really start tithing for a while. I know we've been bringing some meat here, but with as far along as Hannah is, it will make things a great deal easier if we can help them as much as possible," Henri agreed. "Has anyone been assigned to take them meals after the baby is born yet?"

All the women looked at each other. Betty finally answered, "I don't think anyone has thought of it yet."

"I brought a pencil and paper. I'll make sure it happens. I think suppers for a week?"

"That sounds about right," Margaret said.

Henri got up and moved around the circle, asking women which day of the week they preferred, while Emma concentrated on the quilt. Hannah wasn't there, and she couldn't help but wonder why.

Sarah was there with her younger siblings, looking tired, but happy. Her face had a bit of a glow to it, and Emma thought she must be happy in her marriage.

Penelope was excited to be quilting. "I thought when I came west, I would open a seamstress shop. I do love sewing."

"And Herbert doesn't mind when you're not at home working?" Mary asked.

"Not at all," Penelope said. "He's happy that I have time to spend with dear friends I've made along the way."

Trudie nodded, a huge smile on her face. "My Joseph is the same. If Emily is cared for, he's quite happy for me to be among other ladies. It's good we all settled together. If we had been on our own, I'm sure I would have lost my mind."

Emma glanced at Trudie. She'd talked to her a bit at the beginning of their journey west, but the woman had been so prickly, it was difficult to have a conversation with her. Marriage had truly changed her.

All the women seemed pleased to be there, and Hannah came in a short while later. "I'm very sorry I'm late. This morning wasn't a good one."

Mrs. Mitchell shook her head at Hannah. "Most women are over their morning sickness by the time they're three months along. But I've heard it said the more you're sick, the healthier the baby. You will have the healthiest child this side of the Mississippi."

"I'll be thankful for that." Hannah hadn't complained to Emma's knowledge, and she was surprised to learn the other woman was so sick with her pregnancy.

Betty nodded. "Malcom thinks you're doing very well, despite the constant nausea. Just think, in another few weeks, you'll be holding your beautiful baby in your arms. I think that will make it all worth it."

Henri nodded emphatically. "It would be worth it for me."

Emma and her family had all decided to spread themselves out over the entire circle that morning, so if there was little talk, they could keep things moving along. It seemed to be working well.

Just before noon, they all went their separate ways, and Emma started the walk back to their land with Henri and her family. "I have a cold lunch waiting for us at my place," Henri said. "I made bread and I have leftover roast. We'll eat the roast between pieces of bread."

"That sounds good," Emma said. She'd never eaten anything like it, but her mother hadn't made bread, so it made sense she knew so little about it.

They were all out of breath when they got to Henri's cabin, and it was only halfway up the hill. Jared had promised that as it got colder, he'd build a sleigh for them to go in, but for now, they were walking everywhere.

Emma had to stop and stare at the trees for a moment. "Who all is hunting today?" There were two elk, a bear, and several deer. "I know Jared went, and he was hoping for a bear."

Henri shook her head. "He's the only one in our family who ever liked eating bear." Henri opened the front door. "I know Roy was out today, and he said his pa was going with him."

"I think maybe all the men went hunting. That's a lot of meat to process." Emma squared her shoulders. "We should start this afternoon."

"The meat will be better if we let it bleed out for a day or so. We'll work on it tomorrow." Henri looked tired at the mere thought, but there wasn't a single complaint from her lips. She believed it was her job to take care of the men in her life, but she also believed it was a privilege to care for them. Emma couldn't help but admire her attitude.

"We'll start tomorrow then," Emma said. She knew Henri knew better when it came to processing the meat.

That afternoon was spent learning to make pies, and the first thing Henri taught Emma was how to make meat pies. "Does Jared like these?" Emma didn't want to learn to make anything Jared wouldn't be pleased with.

"His two favorite things in the world are chicken and dumplings and meat pies. I probably should have taught you to make this last week."

Emma smiled. "He'll just be happy when I get home then, won't he?"

"I've seen the way my brother looks at you. He's always happy to see you."

"I'm happy to see him as well. I do enjoy being married to your brother." Emma's mother and sisters had gone home after lunch, so it was just the two of them. "I'd like to learn to make fruit pies as well."

"I will teach you. I have some dried apples and some dried cherries left. We'll make a couple of pies with those, and then you'll be able to do it yourself."

"If we write down the receipt for pie crust," Emma said. Henri seemed to remember every receipt she'd ever seen. But Emma wasn't quite as knowledgeable about cooking.

"I think you could follow any receipt you had now, but then I would miss spending time with you, so we won't tell anyone that just yet, and we'll still spend days together. There's no need for either of us to be alone all day, when we're doing the same thing anyway."

"I agree wholeheartedly. How else will we bond as sisters?"

Emma left Henri's house that night with a meat pie, made with elk meat, potatoes, carrots, and a thin gravy. She hadn't had a chance to try it yet, but she knew it was good because she and Henri had made it together.

When she got back to the house, she immediately went out to feed the chickens. There weren't a lot of insects for them to eat as late in the year as it was. So, she sprinkled a bit of stale bread she'd broken into chunks in their little room. It was already starting to stink in there, as chickens always came with a bad smell, but it wasn't unfamiliar to Emma, and she truly didn't mind.

She sometimes tossed them what was left from supper as well. Her ma had taught her that chickens would eat just about anything, and she knew well it was true.

Back in the house, she put the unbaked pie she'd brought from Henri's in the fireplace, atop the Dutch oven. It was best to keep it out of the fire, and way above it for even cooking, according to Henri.

When she was finished with that, she took time to sweep up the house, and dust the few things that needed it. She felt like she had so little to do in her little cabin.

It was a good thing she spent her days with Henri. She would lose her mind from loneliness otherwise, though she did really enjoy coming home for an hour of quiet before Jared got home.

She loved her husband with all her heart, but it was good to have a break after spending an entire day with women, which is what she'd done that day.

When Jared got home, she greeted him with a quick kiss, thankful they were married, and no one would complain if they saw them kissing. "Did you get the bear?"

"I did. No one else in my family likes bear, so they weren't hunting for one. We'll be fed all winter with that one though. He's huge!"

"Henri and I plan to start preserving it tomorrow. I don't know how much we're going to be able to salt, but hopefully enough for us to have a roast once a week or so. Most of it will have to be dried."

He sighed. "I should have gotten it sooner, but it's all right. I do enjoy bear jerky a lot. Have Henri show you how to make it. Hers is better than your ma's."

"It's the only thing my ma can really make that's good."

Smiling, he nodded. "Hers is good. Henri's is better."

"I believe you. I've had Henri's jerky, and it's wonderful. She's much better at seasoning things than my ma is." She walked over to take the pie off the top of the Dutch oven and set it on a cloth on the table.

She'd already set the table and put coffee on the table for both. "I hope you don't mind that Henri and I made meat pies this afternoon…"

"Not if I get one!"

"You're going to have to share one with me. Don't worry, I don't eat very much."

"I've noticed that. Why don't you eat much?"

"I'm not very hungry," she said.

"Ever?"

"I have a good breakfast and a good lunch every single day. I eat supper, but I'm usually not very hungry that late in the day."

Jared smiled. "I'll eat your share and mine too."

"I get a little! I didn't even get to try it yet."

"You have to like it, so you'll cook it for me."

Emma laughed. "Henri said that you love this almost as much as you love chicken and dumplings. I'll learn to make those as soon as I can."

"I wonder how bear would go with dumplings." Jared cocked his head, thinking about it. "Have Henri teach you to make dumplings, and we'll try it with bear meat."

"I will." She rubbed the back of her neck. "We went to the quilting circle at the church today. Our first project is making a quilt for the pastor and Hannah."

"I'm sure that will make them very happy."

Emma nodded. "With that baby coming soon, they're going to need lots of help."

"I can understand that," he said. "We haven't talked about children much. Do you want them?"

She was almost afraid to tell him her real feelings, but she didn't want to lie to him either. "I would like children, but I'd rather we waited a year or two. We won't be able to...enjoy one another as much with a small child."

"And you think our enjoyment of each other is more important than having children right off?"

"Of course, I do. Don't you?"

"I hadn't thought of it that way, honestly. I thought you'd want to have a baby right away like Henri does." He sat for a moment thinking about what she'd said. "I think you're right. Not that we can really control it, but I like the idea of waiting a little while as well. But we must make one another a promise."

"What's that?"

"We cannot be upset if we find we're having a baby sooner. If you discover next month that you're expecting, you must tell me, and we will rejoice over the life God has given us to parent."

"Oh, absolutely. I will love our child no matter what. But I hope we can wait a little while. I do like the idea of having a little boy who looks just like his papa."

He smiled. "And all I can think about is a little girl who is identical to her mama."

"I hope one of us gets their way...eventually."

"How many children would you like?"

"Oh, seven or eight sounds good. Maybe more. Just not next week."

She served them each a portion of the pie, making sure that his was twice the size of hers. As soon as it was on his plate, he gripped her hand and prayed. "I can't believe we wasted all that time talking with meat pie on the table."

She laughed. "It smells good." She cut into it with the side of her fork and lifted it to her mouth. "This is delicious."

"It is. You did a great job!"

"Well, you know I only made the pie crust. I could make it again, though, but that's all I did this time."

"Well, it's wonderful. The pie crust is flaky just as it should be."

"Thanks. It's hard to mess up with Henri right beside me. Though I do think I could duplicate the process since she gave me the receipt for the pie crust. The rest of the meal is easy because of what she's already shown me." Emma looked at him. "Henri said we didn't need bread with this meal, so we didn't make it today. I hope you don't mind."

"Henri's right, as usual. It annoys me how very often she's right. But I'll want bread with my bear stew tomorrow night."

She laughed softly. "I'll make it then. I think we'll be processing meat all day tomorrow. I can't believe how much meat you men brought in."

"We provide the food. All you have to do is cook it," he said.

"That's all?" Emma felt like laughing. He had no idea how much work it was to process that much meat, and it showed. But her mother had once told her that all men think their work is harder than a woman's. She didn't mind.

"You'll make bear stew tomorrow for supper?"

"Absolutely. Would you like carrots and potatoes in it? Over rice or no rice?"

"Since not all the bear meat will be able to be salted and preserved, let's just have stew tomorrow. The more meat the better."

"All right. I'll make sure it happens. I'll bring home a few roasts, and I'll put them in a covered bucket outside where they'll stay cold enough I can make them for several days straight."

Jared grinned, tilting his head to one side. "Imagine how good bear meat pie would be."

"All right. You know, I couldn't cook worth a lick two weeks ago, and here you are, requesting special meals from me."

He chuckled. "I should be shot, but...You'll do it anyway?" At that moment he looked like a small boy begging for a sweet.

"Of course I will. Making you happy is my most important job."

"You make me happy without cooking a single meal. Just looking at you and touching you makes me very happy."

"Well then get to eating. After the dishes are done, we can start the looking and touching portion of our evening." Emma knew her parents read side by side, or Ma would sew while Pa whittled. She had to wonder if they had started their marriage spending their time the way she and Jared did.

"I'm eating! Actually, I've eaten it all. Is there any left?"

"There's still half a pie left. I can give it all to you or just a portion the size that you had the first time. Which would you prefer?"

"All. I'm so happy Henri taught you to make meat pies today. I'll have to tell her so when I see her next."

"For as close as we all live, it's strange you don't see her more. Always on Sundays, but rarely during the week."

He shrugged. "I'm working, and she's working too. It's a different kind of work, and it doesn't bring us together often."

"How would you feel about inviting Roy and Henri to supper on Saturday evening? I'd say for lunch on Sunday, but I don't think you want to give up our alone time."

"I surely don't. Saturday night would be fine. You go to Henri's on Saturdays, don't you?"

She shook her head. "We decided that I should stay home and catch up on housework on Saturdays." Which really meant she spent an hour cleaning, another hour cooking, and she had the rest of the day to herself. It was good to have a day per week when she wasn't surrounded by people.

"It seems to me that you're always caught up with household chores. But what do I know?"

She grinned standing and starting to do the dishes. She was ready for the fun part of their evening to begin.

Chapter Nine

The following evening, Emma made bear meat stew for Jared. She hoped she liked the stew even half as much as he said she would.

She also made a few loaves of bread on her own. Feeling very empowered by her success, she shared some of the meat with Jared's family, as well as enough stew for their supper and lunch the following day.

She set the stew on the hook over the fireplace and left four loaves of bread on the table to go with it. Hopefully the men would like it as much as Jared did.

When she returned home, she found Jared waiting for her. "Are you all right?" she asked.

"I fell and my knee is swollen badly. Pa sent me home and told me to keep my foot up."

She frowned, hurrying to him. "Where did you fall from?" she asked.

"We were all messing around in the loft of the barn, storing stacks of seed up there. Sam pushed me with his shoulder, just playfully, but I lost my balance and fell right over the edge." He shook his head. "I feel like an idiot, and Sam was mortified that he'd actually hurt me."

"Has the doctor seen it?" she asked.

Jared shook his head. "No, I didn't want to bother him with this."

She shook her head. "I'm going to go saddle one of the horses, and I'll ride to get him. He needs to see this. I'm hoping there's something he can do for it."

"I'm sure I just need to rest it and use liniment."

"Let me see it, and I'll decide if you're seeing the doctor." Emma knew she shouldn't be telling her husband what to do, but she also knew he wouldn't see the doctor on his own. She had no idea how she was supposed to help him otherwise.

"Are you asking me to take my pants off, Emma?" he asked, wiggling his eyebrows up and down at her.

"There are very few times I'm not interested in sex with you," Emma said, "but this is one of them. We need to make sure it's all right before you go back to work."

He sighed, unfastening the buttons of his pants, and she helped him remove them. When she saw his knee, it was swollen to double its usual size and a dark purple surrounded it. "What do you think?" he asked.

"I think you need the doctor to look at it. I'll be back shortly. Do you want to have a bowl of stew to eat while I'm gone?" He was in the bed, and normally she didn't like eating in the bed, but she needed to keep him down while she was gone, and it seemed to be the only way.

She put on her winter coat and mittens, wrapping a scarf around her head. It had been below freezing every night since they'd arrived. Everyone was just thankful no snow had lasted more than a day. The ground was hard, but at that point, it wasn't impossible to dig into.

She saddled the smallest of the horses, saying a silent prayer he was easy to ride. She'd only ridden a horse a few times, and now she needed to. Sure, she could go to his family for help, but she felt better going herself. It felt like it was an act of service for him, and she was learning from Henri, that it was best if you enjoy doing for the ones you love.

She went slowly down the hill but picked up the pace when she got to the bottom, heading straight to Dr. Bentley's house. When she got down, she tied the reins to a tree, unsure if this horse would know to stay there or if he or she would return home.

She knocked on the door loudly, praying she wasn't interrupting a night of fun between the doctor and his sweet wife Betty.

Betty came to the door, fully clothed, and that made Emma feel a little better about her unexpected visit. "I'm sorry, but my husband fell from the loft in the barn. His knee is very swollen and black and blue."

"Oh! Malcolm is home. We'll be right there."

"You know where to find us?"

Betty nodded. "We turn just past the church. I've seen the tracks of your wagons."

"All right. I'm going to get there as quickly as I can. I was afraid to leave him alone, but I feel pretty confident he should see the doctor."

"We're coming!" Betty said.

Emma rode quickly up the hill, returning the horse to the barn. She would remember this was a horse who was calm and easy to ride.

Hurrying back to the house, she went inside to find Jared still in bed, but with his bowl of stew gone. "I think I need more," he said, looking at his empty bowl.

Emma laughed. "I'll get you more. The doc and Betty are on their way."

"I think we're disturbing them for nothing," he said.

"If we're only seeing him for my piece of mind, then I'll have to be content with that. Would you like me to bring you some bread and butter as well?"

"Yes, please."

By the time Jared had finished with his second bowl, the Bentleys were there, and the doctor was looking at Jared's knee. "Your wife is right. That doesn't look good. I'm going to give you some laudanum for the pain, and I'll give Emma some liniment for that knee. You need to stay off of it at least until Monday."

"Monday?" Jared grumbled. "No church on Sunday?"

"Not at this point," the doctor said. "Emma, I want him to take the laudanum every four hours for pain. If it's so bad he can't take it, you can move the doses a little closer together."

"I'll do exactly as you say, Dr. Bentley. Thank you for coming."

Dr. Bentley looked at Jared once more. "You're going to be a good patient and listen to your wife, aren't you?"

Jared frowned. "There's so much to do right now. Winter will hit any day."

"I'm aware, but if you ever want to walk without a limp, follow my instructions."

"Yes, sir." Jared was obviously annoyed, but Emma was glad they had instructions for what to do. She felt much safer about him that way.

"I'll do my best to see to it," Emma said. "I know he doesn't want to stay in bed, but it's necessary." She frowned. "Would you stay for supper? I'd feel much better if you did."

Dr. Bentley and Betty exchanged a look. "I already cooked," Betty said softly. "Maybe another time."

"That sounds good." Emma watched the two of them leave and looked at Jared. "Time for your laudanum."

"I don't think I want to take laudanum. Too many people I have known have gotten very sick from it."

Emma had heard many tales about how laudanum turned people into something they weren't before. She didn't want to risk it. Besides, it wouldn't help him heal, it would just help him learn to tolerate pain. "All right. But you'd better not try to go back to work early!" She was certain that was the most important thing for him.

"I'll do my best. Maybe I could sit out front in the morning with a rife at my side. I could at least try to hunt."

She frowned, thinking about it, but finally nodded. Most of the wild creatures wouldn't come close enough to be shot, but it wouldn't hurt him to sit outside with his rifle. "All right, but if you get tired, you need to come inside. I'm going to hurry down the hill and let Henri know I won't be at her house tomorrow."

"Aren't you at least going to keep me company?" he asked.

"I'll bring you your whittling, but then I'll be right back," She took him the small block of wood she'd seen him work on many times as well as a knife. "I'll be back soon. I want to go before it's dark."

She rushed down the hill and explained what was happening to Henri, who volunteered to do the meals for her family all weekend. They hadn't processed nearly enough of the bear meat, so Emma cut off two more large chunks and hurried back up the hill.

As she walked into the cabin, the sun was setting behind her, and it was a glorious sight from atop the hill where they were. The sky was colored with pink, purples, and oranges. It was one of the most beautiful things she'd ever seen, and she was thrilled to know she'd be able to look out at it for the rest of her life.

Hurrying into the house with the bear meat, she found a bucket and just laid the meat outside on the board she'd carried the meat on, with a bucket tipped over on top of it.

Stepping back inside, she looked at Jared. "Do you need anything else? I'm about to try the stew."

"You haven't even tried it yet?" he asked.

"Henri has taught me to taste while I cook, but I wanted you to have the first taste of it, so I decided to wait. Did you like it?"

He nodded. "Best bear stew I've ever had, including Henri's and my ma's. You did a great job with it."

"Thank you," she said, looking forward to her first bite. Henri had warned her that bear may not be to her taste, but she was determined to try it. Filling a bowl, she carried a chair over next to the bed, so she could chat with Jared while he slept.

She held her bowl in her hands, bowed her head for a silent prayer, and took her first bite. "Oh! This is good! It tastes like sweet venison."

"I'm glad you like it. Now I can get a bear every fall, and we'll eat happily all winter."

She smiled. "I have a feeling we'll both want a little more variety than that, but we'll see." Emma really liked to eat chicken, and if they could get some roosters the following year, they'd have them for meals. They only needed one for their flock to keep growing anyway.

"Maybe you will, but bear meat is my favorite, and I could eat it every day for the rest of my life." Jared looked adamant, and he looked up from his whittling and waved his knife at her.

She wasn't going to argue with him about the best kind of meat, so she changed the subject. "After I've eaten, I'll apply the liniment. Can you think of anything else that would keep you busy?" she asked.

"I wouldn't mind if you brought me the Bible. I need to read. Just sitting here whittling, I'll get bored, not pay attention, and cut one of my fingers off. Then you'll have to go riding down the hill to get the doctor again. It's just not wise."

She shook her head but couldn't help but smile at his silliness. "I'll make sure you have the Bible beside you. I'll be here as well, so if you think of anything else, I can help."

Emma finished eating and washed the dishes, sweeping the floors, and looking around for something else to clean. When she found nothing else was dirty, she moved back to the chair at his side. She brought the baby gown she was making for Henri along with her.

Instead of reading or whittling, Jared watched her sew the lace onto the collar of the little gown. "Who is that for?"

"Henri."

"Is she already expecting?" he asked with shock in his voice.

She shook her head. "No, but I try to always keep a few baby gowns made up for friends who have babies. I'm saying this one is for Henri, but it may be for us. I don't know."

"I certainly don't want to have a baby before they do," he said. "Though I know Henri would welcome a baby tomorrow."

Emma smiled. "I'm sure it's not a contest to see who will have a baby first. Does your pa want to be a grandfather?"

"Pa doesn't talk about things like that, but Ma wanted a grandchild more than anything." Emma could see the sadness on Jared's face when he talked about his ma.

"Tell me about your ma. What was she like?"

He shrugged. "She was a loving mother. A good wife to Pa. She was a wonderful cook, but she hated to sew. She kept her house perfectly neat, and once chased me with a broom when I tracked mud into the house. I never really thought about what she was like because she was my ma. Does that make sense?"

"It does. I'm sure you miss her every day."

"I sure don't miss her like Henri does. She and Ma were super close, and they did everything together. Henri likes the things Ma liked, and she dislikes the things Ma disliked. She acts like she's just fine, and she may be now, but right after it happened, we'd hear her crying at night. No one knew what to say or do, so we all pretended we didn't hear it."

"Oh, that's so sad," Emma said, tying off her thread. "I know I'd be devastated if I lost my ma."

"Hopefully that won't happen any time soon." He patted the bed beside him. "I think you should get undressed and join me."

Emma frowned. "You can't try to make love with me. We might hurt your knee."

"It would be worth it!"

"No, it wouldn't. Monday, when you go back to work, we can resume our fun evenings. For now, we're just going to have to use a little self-control."

Jared looked downright ornery at her words. He obviously didn't think he was hurt badly enough that he should have to restrain himself. "I know how my knee feels better than you do."

Emma nodded. "That's very true. Oh, I forgot your liniment." She jumped up and brought the little pot of medicine to him. When she was back by his side, he wouldn't even look at her. She ignored his attitude and carefully smoothed the liniment all over the swelling and bruising of his knee. "There you go. Hopefully it will make it better faster."

"I know what would make it better faster," he said, trying one last time to get his way.

"I will not help you hurt yourself," Emma said, putting the liniment back on the table where she'd left it.

She turned down the lanterns and undressed, pulling one of her old nightdresses on before climbing into bed with him. She was careful not to touch him in any way, as she could feel his anger emanating from him.

Lying there in the silence, she prayed for sleep. She didn't want to have to argue with him about whether or not he should pay attention to what the doctor had said or not. Carefully, so as not to jostle him too much, she turned on her side away from him.

Their first fight. She knew it would come because every couple fought at times, but she wasn't ready for it yet. She was sure it would take them years to have their first fight, and here they were a week and a half into their marriage. She was angry back at him.

She had saddled a horse, ridden down the hill to fetch the doctor, and ridden back up. Perhaps for him it would have been a leisurely ride, but for an inexperienced rider, it had been incredibly difficult. But he wouldn't open his eyes and realize what she'd done.

She sighed dramatically, telling her brain to sleep. There was no point in letting him bother her when she knew she'd done everything she could for him.

HENRI CAME UP THE NEXT morning to tell her they wouldn't be coming for supper the next evening. Emma stepped outside with her. "I don't mind cooking for you."

Henri nodded. "I know you don't, but I happen to know my brother and how he acts when he's sick or injured. No one should have to be around him. I almost think you should move back in with your parents and make Sam take care of him."

Emma smiled, pleased to hear he was simply a poor patient. She'd worried he was angry with her. Well, he probably still was a little angry with her, but that was just fine with her. He'd get past it. "I'm glad you told me that. He's been grumbling and angry with me, and I thought I was being a bad wife."

Henri shook her head. "Oh, not at all. He's just a big baby when he's sick. All of my brothers are. Pa too, come to think of it. Ma would always put whoever was sick into their room, and she'd make regular visits to see if they needed anything, but then she'd walk right out if they started fussing at her. I wish you had a room you could put him in, so you didn't have to listen to him."

"I like how your mother handled it. I will do that once we have a real house and not just a simple log cabin. For now, I think I may stick some cotton in my ears, so I can't hear him complaining. It would be a horrible thing to do, but it would feel so good."

Henri laughed. "I think that's the perfect solution. Just make sure you feed him three times a day and use whatever medication the doc left for him."

"Trust me. I will."

"I'm going to go keep working on putting up the meat. Did you like the bear?" Henri asked.

"I loved it. I don't know about for every meal all winter, but I enjoyed it very much."

"It's all yours then. Bear jerky, bear roasts. Whatever you want to do with it. In fact, why don't I bring you some of the meat to turn into jerky today. I'll write down how I do it, and you can just get started. He can't complain when you're making sure he has meat for the entire winter."

"I like that idea!" Emma said, thankful to learn this was just how Jared was when he was sick. She could make it until Monday with that knowledge.

Chapter Ten

By Monday morning when Jared was allowed to go back to work, Emma was fed up with him. She had no desire to even look at the man, much less do anything that would please him.

She made pancakes for breakfast, and though she fixed his plate as always, she didn't speak to him while doing so. She took her spot at the table, and she didn't hold his hand when he prayed over the meal.

She was half finished with her breakfast when he looked at her in surprise. "Are you angry with me?"

Emma blinked a few times as she looked at him. "You haven't been the best patient."

"Oh, that? Isn't everyone crabby when they're sick?"

"It seems to me you could win a crabbiness award for how you behaved over the past three days." Emma didn't want to fight with him, but she felt she at least deserved an apology with the way he'd acted.

"And that means you're angry with me?" He seemed truly confused as to what her problem was.

"You yelled at me more than once. You told me I was doing the jerky incorrectly, even though I was following your sister's instructions exactly. Then you told me you were surprised it was edible because I'd done it wrong. You complained when I let you sit out front with your rifle. You complained when I let you stay in bed. In fact, if I had listened to you, I would believe that there was nothing at all good about me, and I didn't deserve to be married to you, much less live." Emma took a deep breath to calm down. "This entire time has been infuriating to me. I kept my temper. I did as you asked whenever you asked. But I didn't deserve to be treated as you treated me. I was certain I was in a perfect marriage, and now I must wonder why I even speak with you."

He stared at her for a moment. "Was I really that bad?" he asked.

"You were worse. Never in my life have I seen someone so completely selfish over an injury that he couldn't be civil to the woman who was taking care of him. I will not be treated as if I'm a bug stuck to the bottom of your shoe."

She stood up and started to wash the dishes, not even wanting to look at him for another moment.

Jared sat for a moment and tried to remember all the things he'd said to her, and he frowned. His mother had always told him he was particularly intolerable when he was ill or injured, but he'd never considered exactly what she was talking about. Now he knew.

"I'm sorry," he said softly. He hated having done something that would make him have to say it, but he knew he was in the wrong.

"Until the next time you're ill?" she asked, not yet ready to forgive his ridiculous behavior.

"I'll do better next time. I truly didn't realize I was as bad as what you're saying. I truly am sorry. I hope you can find it in your heart to forgive me."

"Of course, I'll forgive you. I love you. But I don't enjoy being treated that way, and then next time it happens, I will stay with my parents, and you will be on your own trying to figure out food and learning to deal with whatever is wrong all by yourself."

Jared stared at her for a moment. "You love me? You've never said that before."

"No, I haven't, and I don't know if I was ready to say it now. You make me want to pound my head against the wall in frustration at the same time as I want to beg you to make love with me. You thought it was so hard to go all weekend without our lovemaking. Did it ever occur to you it was difficult for me as well?"

He got to his feet, limping only slightly as he approached her. "I won't treat you that way again. I love you as well, and I never want you to feel like I don't." He pulled her into his arms, and she only resisted for a moment before she melted against him.

"It's hard to stay angry with you," she said, resting her head on his shoulder.

"I won't hurt you again. I promise."

She laughed. "Of course you will. People always hurt the people they love most. Now that I know you love me, I hope I will be able to take it better than I did this time."

He sighed. "I wish I could spend more time with you today, but I have to get to work."

"And I have meat to process with your sister." She moved away from him. "I'm going to neaten the cabin, and then I'll work with her all day. Are you going to eat lunch with your brothers and father?"

"That's the plan," he said. He kissed her deeply. "I'll be thinking of you all day."

And then he was gone.

True to her word, Emma swept the cabin, made the bed, and made sure everything was right back where it belonged, and then she started the walk down the hill. The ground still wasn't frozen, and she was thankful for that, but it was going to happen any day. She could feel it in the air.

When she got to Henri's, the two of them began working together quickly, with the ease of knowing how to anticipate one another. "Roy made me several barrels to preserve food in. We'll still soak it in brine, and then pack salt around it, but we'll make a barrel of bear meat, and a barrel of elk, and so on. We'll have the men take the bear meat to your house."

Emma laughed. "I enjoyed the bear meat. Probably more than I should have. We'll happily take it. Jared has already given me a list of foods that he loves that he wants me to try it in. Including bear meat and dumplings, so I'll have to get your receipt for dumplings."

"That sounds disgusting to me, but if it's what he wants... You can try it once, and if neither of you like it, never make it again. Even the best cook will have some failures when she is experimenting with different foods."

"I'll do what I can. I don't care if I don't like it because I've never had your chicken and dumplings and can't quite comprehend how good they're supposed to be."

Henri smiled. "You'll love chicken and dumplings. Actually, I've found that both you and your brother love any food that's prepared well. I think he'd love bear meat if I made it for him, but I'm not fond of bear meat, so I won't do that."

Emma laughed softly. "After spending my entire eighteen years eating things that were burned or cooked incorrectly in a dozen different ways, I find I do enjoy most food. Prepare it well, and I will not complain about eating it. I never complained about Ma's food either, though."

"You're a better person than I am. I've become rather picky. If it's food, and I'm hungry, I'll eat it, but I won't necessarily be happy about it, if that makes sense. There are some foods that just don't taste good to me, and I know my brothers are as picky as I am. It comes from always having well-prepared meals." Henri smiled. "Other than our first week or two on the trail when all the bread Ma and I could make turned out horribly. We would throw it out, and it would still be there the following morning, which means even the animals wouldn't eat it."

Emma giggled. "That makes me like you so much more than I already do. You haven't always cooked everything perfectly. It makes you more human in my eyes."

"What was I before?" Henri asked. "A rat?"

"No, of course not. You just seemed to be above the rest of us. Never making mistakes. I like you better now that I know you do make mistakes on occasion."

"I'm sure Jared could tell you stories about me and how I messed things up. They certainly won't be forgotten by me."

"They have been by Jared. He really thinks you do no wrong. It's hard to live up to his expectations for me after having grown up with you."

Henri thought about it for a moment and said, "I'm so sorry. You don't need something like that troubling you at the start of your marriage."

"It's not your fault. You are who you were raised to be, and I'm feeling insecure. It's not you at all."

"Well, I think you are a perfect bride for my oldest brother. Jared is difficult at times, as I'm sure you learned this weekend, but he's a good man through and through."

"Thank you, Henri. For helping my confidence and for teaching me so many things that would help me be a better wife. Without you, we'd be eating poorly cooked meals and jerky and nothing else."

"Oh!" Henri said, "That reminds me that I wrote out all my receipts for you in an old journal. I want you to have it as my wedding present to you."

"Thank you so much! Now you won't have to put up with me in your home every single day."

Henri smiled. "I hope you won't quit coming. Your friendship has come to mean a lot to me. We're sisters now."

"I won't quit coming unless the weather gets much worse than it is right now. Wouldn't it be nice if we didn't get much snow this winter at all? And we were all worried about it for no reason?"

"It would be wonderful if that happened, but I have a feeling it's not something that we'll run into. Not ever."

Emma sighed. "Probably not. But all of our winter preparations are going to hold us over. I'm sure of it."

Henri nodded. "I think we have the meat we need for the winter and then some. We'll be able to share with families who are low on food."

"I need to learn to make beans yet. I always covered them with water to cook, but Ma told me I was being wasteful of the little water we had. She put a little water in the bottom of the pot, and put the lid on, and hers came out terribly crunchy, and not at all appetizing."

Henri shook her head. "You were doing it right. To make beans, I cover them with water to soak them in the morning on the day I will cook them. Then I dump that water out and refill with water. Then I cook them, making sure they are always covered with water. I season them with salt, and serve over rice."

"That sounds easy."

"It is one of the easiest meals you can make. My men got sick of it, but Ma and I purchased two different types of beans, and most families only had one type. But you do the same basic thing with all of them."

Emma smiled. "I think I can do that."

They continued processing the meat as they talked to one another. This was the biggest task they had before winter set in, and both were determined to do it well. "All we ate this weekend was bear," Emma said. "We had bear meat pie, bear stew, bear soup, and even a bear roast. Jared is convinced we can eat bear every day this winter and never get bored with it."

Henri grinned. "I'm not so sure about that!"

"I told him the same thing, but he's certain of it. I'm glad I like the meat, though, or my winter would be intolerable."

On her walk home that afternoon, Emma decided to make the bear meat and dumplings Jared had wanted to try so badly.

She would follow Henri's receipt exactly, other than switching out bear meat for the chicken. She'd said some things that morning that had needed to be said, but she still felt terrible for saying them.

This would be a way she could make an apology and assuage her feelings without backing down on what she'd said.

When Jared came back for supper, her first question was to ask him how his knee was.

"Oh, it's better than it was. I'm still moving a little slower than I'd like, but I was able to keep up with my brothers, and we got a bit more hunting done."

"It seems to me, we've moved to an area where hunting is plentiful!" Emma said. "Henri and I were just saying today that we were certain we had enough food for the winter. Anything else killed, we'll share with others. I think I'm taking a bit of the bear meat down to the doc and Betty on Sunday. I can give it to them at church."

"That's a good idea. And I know our tithing this winter is supposed to be in food. We can take some to the Scotts as well."

"I'll ask around for the names of people who need a little help this winter, and we'll get them some meat as well." Emma liked the idea of sharing their bounty hunting-wise with the community. It was a way for them to thank everyone who had helped along the way.

After supper dishes were done, Jared pulled her into his arms and held her close. "I couldn't stop thinking about what you said this morning all day. I will do everything I can to never treat you that way again. I hope you know that."

She nodded. "I do believe you. Besides, I've heard that kissing and making up was the best way to get through an argument."

He chuckled. "I think we're going to need to give that a try." When his mouth came down on hers, her arms wrapped around him.

"I love you so much," Emma told him.

"I love you as well. Now stop talking and let's go to bed!"

Epilogue

Emma found that God was on her side when a year passed, and then another, and she didn't find herself pregnant. She was starting to get antsy when they realized it was their second anniversary, and they were settled into their house, and she still wasn't expecting.

Everyone else seemed to be having babies. Henri was the mother of one child and expecting the next, but Emma just couldn't seem to get pregnant.

One evening she mentioned to Jared that she worried she might be barren, and he shook his head. "We said two years. It's two years today. I'm sure you'll be expecting within a month or two."

JARED WAS RIGHT. THEIR baby was born exactly nine months from their second anniversary. Emma had prayed for a son who would be just like his father, but instead, she had a beautiful little girl, who looked nothing like her father.

After her mother and Mrs. Mitchell had left, Emma sat staring into the tiny face with wonder. "I'm so glad she was born in the summer and not the winter," Emma said. Winters there were not for the faint of heart.

"I am too. You'll be able to take her to Henri's and introduce her to her cousins soon."

"Her double cousins," Emma reminded him. "I'm thrilled we have this beautiful child. Now we need to make more."

"You need to heal first."

"I do. But I don't want her to be an only child for long." Emma frowned. "What will we name her? We can't call her baby forever."

"Oh, we could, but it would be terribly unkind of us."

"I agree," Emma said.

"What would you think of naming her Annabelle? It's a name I've always liked."

"Perfect. Shall we call her Annie or Belle?"

"I like Belle," Jared said. "Our own beautiful daughter."

"I'm so glad we have a proper house, and I won't be trying to cook over an open fire with a baby in the house. Life is so much easier now than it was that first winter."

"I still like the first winter best," Jared told her. "That's when we fell in love."

"And we'll never fall out," she said, grinning at him. "You should hold her, Papa."

Jared felt a wave of emotion at being called Papa. Now he felt as if his family was complete. Oh, they'd add other children along the way, but this one...it made them parents, and they were going to be the best parents around.

If you enjoyed this book, make sure you go back and read about all the people mentioned in the Clover Creek Caravan series.

To get notice of new books by Kirsten Osbourne, click here[1].

---

1. http://www.kirstenandmorganna.com/newsletter

Ingram Content Group UK Ltd.
Milton Keynes UK
UKHW011807040723
424531UK00004B/281